# SANTA LOVES CURVY GIRLS

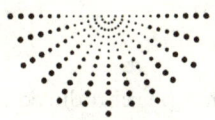

## KELSIE STELTING

Copyright © 2024 by Kelsie Stelting

All rights reserved.

No part of this book may be reproduced in any form or by any electronic or mechanical means, including information storage and retrieval systems, without written permission from the author, except for the use of brief quotations in a book review.

This is a work of fiction. Names, characters, businesses, places, events, locales, and incidents are either the products of the author's imagination or used in a fictitious manner. Any resemblance to actual persons, living or dead, or actual events is purely coincidental.

For questions, address kelsie@kelsiestelting.com.

Editing by Tricia Harden

Proof Reading by Jordan Truex

Cover design by Najla Qamber Designs

**Readers sensitive to certain types of content should visit https://kelsiebooks.com/pages/sensitive-content to learn more.**

❀ Created with Vellum

*For all my curvy girls who want to be the star of a Christmas romance—this one's for you.*

# CONTENTS

1. Belle — 1
2. Nick — 9
3. Belle — 16
4. Nick — 23
5. Belle — 29
6. Nick — 34
7. Belle — 39
8. Nick — 47
9. Belle — 53
10. Nick — 61
11. Nick — 68
12. Belle — 74
13. Nick — 79
14. Belle — 85
15. Nick — 89
16. Belle — 94
17. Nick — 99
18. Belle — 106
19. Nick — 113
20. Belle — 117
21. Nick — 122
22. Belle — 128
23. Nick — 133
24. Belle — 138
25. Nick — 146
26. Belle — 153
27. Nick — 158
28. Belle — 162
29. Nick — 170

| *Author's Note* | 175 |
| *Acknowledgments* | 179 |
| *About the Author* | 181 |
| *Also by Kelsie Stelting* | 183 |

# 1
# BELLE

*G*arland, Maine was a special place where you could make a wish once a year when they put the star on the Christmas tree in the town square. More often than not, my wishes had come true.

Other than Christmas Day, it was my favorite day of the year.

As I finished getting ready, I looked in the mirror and fixed my candy-cane-red scarf. It stood out against my dark wavy hair. Then I checked the rest of my reflection. Tonight, I'd worn a form-fitting green sweater dress instead of an outfit that would hide my extra curves and wide-calf knee-high boots. Before I could second guess my appearance, I turned and headed down the stairs.

I'd never missed the star being placed on the tree, not since I was a little kid who sat on my dad's shoulders, and I definitely wasn't going to miss it this year.

I checked the time on my phone. My friends had to be on their way too. I tapped out a quick text as I left my house, letting Mom know I'd be at the town square.

The holidays were always a busy time in Garland, more so in December with thousands of tourists coming to town. There was so much to do, from volunteering at Santa's Elves to going on sleigh rides or working at the Snowed Inn Lodge.

Not to mention finding someone cute to kiss at Mistletoe Hill.

I'd done just about everything there was to do in Garland except for that last particular attraction. Not that it was an official attraction. More like the secret make-out spot the local kids went to.

You had to have a cute boy invite you there, and I was just not the kind of girl who got those invites. Neither were my friends. We weren't the right size or fit into the right crowds at school. Something I'd sadly realized as early as elementary school.

But that was another reason I had to get to Cider Center, where the big Christmas tree stood.

This year would be different. I could feel it in my bones. I had a very special wish to make this time around as the star lit up.

By the time I got to Cider Center, the crowds were bustling and murmuring with excitement.

"Excuse me," I said politely as I made my way to the front. Even though I was shivering and I could see my breath, I wouldn't trade being here for anything.

This was my moment.

There was something about the Christmas season that made it so the cold could reach my nose and fingers but my heart felt big, hopeful, and warm.

It was the season of miracles, wishes, and gift-giving. Anything was possible.

"Belle!" I heard someone call nearby.

I turned around, trying to find the person behind the familiar voice.

Holly's bright brown eyes came into view among the sea of Garland locals and tourists.

"Holly!" I yelled. The crowds were getting louder now. People squeezed and jostled, trying to make it near the front for a good view. In just a minute, the tree would light up, officially kicking off the Christmas season in our little town.

She waved and smiled, our other friends in tow.

"I'm so glad you guys made it." I hopped on my toes a little, trying to stay warm.

The girls lined up on either side of me.

Carolynn was the last to arrive. "Wouldn't miss it," she said, although I may have detected a hint of sarcasm.

"I've got five minutes before I've gotta run, but I didn't want to miss this either," Bethany said.

Sera was still in her work uniform. "Hi, Belle, looking cute."

Carolynn, Bethany, Holly, and Sera. My ride or die group of best friends since elementary school.

And like me, plus size and desperately single.

"When's your cousin getting here?" I asked Sera.

"Tomorrow, and I hear she's real thrilled," she replied, sarcasm dripping from her voice.

Before I could ask her what her cousin had done to get sent here for Christmas, the ceremony began.

Whispers of excitement filled the air around us

as everyone turned their eyes up toward the Christmas tree in front of us.

The Garland Christmas tree stood well over thirty feet tall, covered in so many lights and ornaments that you could hardly see the evergreen branches underneath.

Legend has it that the tree was harvested at the North Pole each year, which is why magic traveled through the leaves and branches all the way up to the star and made so many Garland Christmas wishes come true.

The mayor of Garland always did the honors. With the help of a fire truck ladder, he made his way up, up, up toward the very tip of the tree. Little kids screamed and laughed and pointed. The mayor waved down at them.

When he reached the top, he pulled out a microphone, the large star under his other arm. "It's the most wonderful time of the year," he said, echoing the familiar song. "Today, it's my honor as your mayor to place the star on the tree and light up Garland, knowing that the holiday spirit of the people of our town shines brighter than any light on this tree."

This was it. My heart sped up with anticipation.

As the light of the star came on, I clasped my hands together and closed my eyes, whispering my wish to myself but praying it was heard by Garland Christmas magic.

Whoever was up there approving Christmas miracles in Garland, Maine, I hoped they saw how important this was, not just for me but for my friends, too.

I wish for my friends and me to fall in love by the new year.

Maybe it was a reach. No, it was *definitely* a reach. Especially with how hard dating seemed to be at my size. But I believed. I had to. This felt like my only shot to fall in love before graduating high school, so I was going to take it.

Long ago, the Garland Christmas magic had worked for my dad when he wished my mom would go out with him. Maybe today it would work for me too.

"Belle, look at it. Isn't it so pretty?" Holly said quietly.

I opened my eyes. The star glowed a bright yellow white, along with the colorful lights on the tree. We stood there, mesmerized.

People around us began clapping and cheering, and we joined in.

Bethany wiped a tear from the corner of her eye. "This part always makes me cry." I put my arm around her shoulder, feeling exactly the same way.

This was the reason I'd never leave Garland.

While the crowds around us dispersed, we instinctively stood in a circle to keep warm and close to each other.

"Wish for anything special this year?" Carolynn asked.

I opened my mouth, unsure if I should say.

Then Sera jumped in. "Just that we remain friends like this forever. No matter what."

I grinned. "That's a great wish."

Holly glanced toward Santa's Workshop down the street. "So, who do you think will be picked to be Santa this year?"

Getting selected was both a secret and a huge honor here in Garland. No one even really knew for sure how you got nominated or how you applied. That's what a big deal it was for no one to know the secret identity of Santa Claus.

Carolynn shrugged. "Maybe they'll pick Mr. Thornton."

We shuddered. Mr. Thornton was our middle-aged math teacher. He certainly had the right belly to be Santa. But we liked to say he had more of the spirit of the Grinch than the cheer required to be Santa.

Before we went our separate ways, we kept making guesses, each one more and more crazy.

As we reached Cocoa Corner, the local coffee shop, we all got ready to head in different directions.

"He just better not be someone's creepy old grandpa," Sera said.

We laughed. I crossed my fingers like I was wishing for good luck. "I sure hope not."

"See you next week!" Holly waved before crossing the street. Sera and Carolynn did the same. I waved after them. With all of us working part-time jobs for the holiday and this being the busiest time of the year, we wouldn't be able to hang out again until after Christmas when we met up at our classmate Haley's big New Year's Eve party.

And if my wish came true (please come true) there'd be plenty to fill each other in about. A girl could dream.

## 2
## NICK

"See you at Haley's New Year's party?" Kane asked as we parted ways after the lighting of the Christmas tree.

I hesitated. "Um, maybe. I'll text you?" With one last wave, I made my way back home.

While I played on the football team at school, Kane was our resident star pitcher. Most of the school jocks would be at Haley's big holiday party this weekend. The cheerleaders too. But what I really wanted was to spend some time away from everyone.

It was pressure enough during football season, knowing everyone's eyes were on me. What I wanted this Christmas was a chance to be someone different.

Play a different role than the one I had always played.

That's why I'd asked my dad if he'd ever been picked to be Santa in Garland.

Getting to be Santa Claus was a huge deal in this town, and the rule was that no one could know who it was. Even now, Dad wouldn't tell me, but I had a sneaking suspicion he'd been selected back in his day.

Let's just say I'd noticed one year in Mom's photo album when Garland Santa and Dad had never been in the same room. I'd never be able to ask him and find out for sure, though, and Mom always got kind of weepy if he came up. The holidays were a tough time for her.

I bet it paid good money to be the official Santa in Garland. Every winter, I took on as many small jobs as I could for my college fund. Shoveling driveways, chopping firewood, that kind of thing. I'd even played Santa Claus at the mall a couple towns over last year. Anything where I could get away from the spotlight for once.

The guys on the team were nice—and so were the cheerleaders—but it also felt like none of them really saw me for me.

A couple minutes later, I walked into Santa's

Elves. I liked to come in here around this time of year to see if there was anything I could do to help. When my mom came upon hard times after my dad died, this place had really helped us out for a few months. I'd been too little to know what was going on, but I still remembered shopping for groceries in the food pantry in the back. The presents I'd unwrapped under the tree that year had come from here too. Santa's Elves was there for any family in Garland who needed a little extra help.

Whether it was mopping the floors, hauling away junk, or reading books to little kids, they usually had something for me to do, and tonight was no different.

Mrs. Mulberry's eyes twinkled up at me from behind her glasses. "I don't know what we're going to do without you once you're off to college next year, Nick."

I smiled and picked up the heavy box she wanted me to move to the basement. "Oh, you'll just have to keep putting up with me, ma'am. I'll be here every winter break. You can count on it."

That was if I ended up making it to my number one choice. The state university wasn't cheap, but my grades were decent and I could throw a football. I had a chance of snagging some sort of scholarship.

After I finished moving boxes, I came back upstairs. "Anything else I can help you with, Mrs. Mulberry?" I asked, leaning forward on the counter.

"You're wonderful, sweetie," she said. She was sorting through food donations. "That's all."

Before I could ask if she wanted help stocking all that stuff in the pantry, she spoke up again. "Oh, by the way, I hear there's a package you need to sign for at the post office, hon."

My brow crinkled. "A package? Are they open now?"

She nodded. "They always work extra hours around the holidays to get everyone's packages shipped out. Mr. Long called about an hour ago. He knows you come here on Saturdays."

Mr. Long was about ninety-five years old, and he still worked at the Garland Post Office.

"Okay," I said, wondering what kind of package was waiting for me. It would be a first. "I'll head over there then."

"Merry Christmas, sweetie," she said with a smile that made her eyes crinkle.

"Have a merry Christmas, Mrs. Mulberry," I replied.

The post office was only a few streets over. I was there in no time, especially because I had no idea who would be sending me a package.

We didn't usually get gifts from relatives or anything. And anyway, wouldn't those come to our house?

I walked in. It was packed, as it always was this time of year. There was a long line of people, all holding packages of various sizes.

Mr. Long was at the front, slowly ringing up Ms. Jane, who worked at the library.

"Nick!" he said, spotting me. "I've got something for you."

With that, he ran to the back and returned a minute later with a large brown package in his hands. "This is for you."

I took it. "But I'm not expecting anything."

I noticed some wording. "To be opened only by Nick St. James." I saw there wasn't a return address either, but Mr. Long was already back to helping the next person in line, so I couldn't ask about it.

The box was big enough that I wondered what could be inside. It wasn't super heavy. I could carry it home no problem, but what was it?

As I made my way home, I took guesses. It was too big to be a new video game console. Plus, I wasn't really into video games. Mom would never go for it anyway.

Maybe Mom had ordered something else for me, but that had me feeling a little guilty. I didn't want her spending money on expensive gifts for me. If anything, she deserved something nice, not me.

I made it home and closed the door behind me. Mom wouldn't be home until later, so the house was quiet. I walked past our goldfish in the living room and headed to my room.

After I set the box on my bed, I took a step back, still wondering what it could be. Only one way to find out.

I found a box cutter in the junk drawer in the kitchen and went back to the box.

Time to find out what this thing was.

The box cutter sliced neatly through the packaging tape. I opened up the box, and my jaw fell open.

No way.

"No way, no way, no way," I said to myself.

Was this…

I held up the large red suit with fluffy white

trimming. There was even a sturdy black pair of boots in here. And a hat.

When I pulled out the hat, a small white note fell out.

*Garland Mall, 3pm on Sunday.*

*Keep the secret. Keep the magic alive.*

I set the note down and looked at the Santa suit on my bed.

It would be me. I was this year's Santa Claus.

3
BELLE

My favorite thing about the holidays (after the lighting of the tree) was the baking.

The house smelled great and stayed warm all day long after I made a big batch of Christmas cookies.

"Here comes Santa Claus, here comes Santa Claus," I sang under my breath, "right down Santa Claus Lane."

I finished frosting the very last cookie, the music still blasting from the Bluetooth speaker in the kitchen. It had been a gift from my little brother, Dylan, last year. He was an eighth grader and pretty sweet when he wasn't being a complete doofus with his friends.

Standing back and looking at my work, I nodded. My grandma's sugar cookie recipe never failed me. Two dozen almost perfect cookies lay on the counter, an assortment of Christmas trees, presents, and even a Mr. and Mrs. Claus. This was my best batch yet.

Yeti came up to me, her little bark letting me know she wanted a treat too.

I kneeled down and scratched the fluffy white fur behind her ears. "No, girl, these cookies aren't for you."

She barked again, indignant, her black little nose in the air.

"Fine," I replied. Yeti knew I lacked the self-discipline to tell her no to a treat.

I stood back up and reached for a treat in the cabinet.

Now she did her happy bark.

"Oh, now you love me," I teased. After some more pets and letting her eat her treat, I packed up the cookies and headed to the mall.

Today was the first day that this year's Santa Claus would be at the mall. It was a very big deal. There were always elves, a beautiful winter backdrop, and a long line of overly excited kids waiting to tell Santa what they wanted for Christmas.

I knew for a fact that some of those kids were also on the naughty list this year, but that was not my business as the official cookie maker of the operation.

My job was to bring the cookies and the holiday spirit, then I'd settle in at Cocoa Corner with some hot chocolate and a few of my favorite baking blogs.

When I walked into the mall, chaos was already underway.

I walked up to my mom, who had a clipboard in hand. She was the general manager at the mall that surrounded the town square, and this was always her craziest time of year. "No," she said sternly, "the line has to start over here." She pointed to the masking tape on the floor. "We went over this yesterday, everyone. Let's get it together."

This was not a good sign. Santa Claus wasn't even sitting in his armchair yet, and already there were little kids running around the stage area, yelling and screaming like they were on the playground.

Plus, Mom was already yelling, and I could see her forehead vein.

"Anything I can help with, Mom?" I asked, still holding the cookies.

She turned to me with a look of relief. "Belle, you're here, thank goodness." She took the cookies from me and gave them to one of her assistants rushing past.

The assistant gave her a confused look but decided to take the cookies and keep walking.

Mom kept her eyes on me. "I need an elf."

"Huh?" I'm sure she didn't even notice my puzzled look. She was already dragging me to the back.

We walked into her office. "Sarah called in sick an hour ago, and we're already short on elves as it is this year."

She pulled an elf suit from a rack near the wall and shoved it into my arms. "Here. Be ready to go in five minutes."

Five minutes?

Before I could say another word, she was gone.

I'd never seen her this stressed out before. Poor Mom. I made a note to make her a special cup of hot chocolate at home later.

But for now, it looked like I was gonna have to step in.

Whether I wanted to or not.

I held up the elf costume, all red and green with tights and a short skirt.

Who made this thing?

The good news was that Sarah and I were about the same size. The bad news was that this costume probably hadn't been dry-cleaned since Mom had started working here. And that was ages ago.

I sighed.

There were little kids and families out there who came to experience some Christmas magic today.

I didn't realize I'd be a part of it when I woke up this morning, but that was life as the oldest daughter of the manager of the Garland Mall. Just last year I'd gotten stuck spraying fake snow on all the shop windows. And the year before that, I had to help dispose of reindeer poop from Santa's petting zoo. (Good thing the live animals weren't coming back this year. That was a mess."

After making a quick change in the ladies' room, I checked myself out in the mirror.

My legs didn't look half bad in this bright green elf skirt and candy-striped tights. As long as you ignored the way the top tugged around my stomach and arms.

And I could certainly do without the little gold bells on the neckline and the pointy hat.

After dabbing on some lip gloss from Mom's purse and doing the best I could for my hair, I stepped out, ready for a day of corralling kids, watching for line-cutters, and threatening to report rule-breakers to the naughty list.

"Oh, honey, you look adorable!" Mom said. "You're my hero for stepping in today."

Before I could chime in, letting her know she owed me a cup of hot cocoa, she was running off again.

I spotted my cookies under some tinsel at the table next to Santa's armchair. Then I walked over there to rescue them.

"Who put these here?" I said to myself. I made quick work of organizing the table so it didn't look such a mess.

A few other elves roamed around. One got the line of kids in order. Another one took a seat at the registration table where a couple of moms were waiting to sign their kids up for pictures with Santa.

Mom called the first kid in the line forward. The show was getting started, and I needed to get out of the way. Santa would be here any—

As I spun and attempted to walk in that direction, I hit something hard.

Hard, yet red and soft.

Before I could fall back, he caught me.

"Whoa there," he said, his voice deep and strong.

He helped me regain my balance.

Bright blue eyes stared down at me. I couldn't see the rest of his face behind the thick white beard—and the thick white eyebrows too—but I could tell from the way his eyes crinkled that he was smiling.

I froze, unable to form words all of a sudden.

I'd bumped straight into Santa Claus.

# 4
# NICK

*F*or a guy who was supposed to be married to Mrs. Claus, I sure didn't expect to have a very pretty elf in my arms as part of this gig.

As she got her bearings, I let her go.

"Hi," she said, still wide-eyed.

"Hi," I replied. I couldn't help but smile down at her, noticing her wavy brown hair beneath the red and green striped hat and her pretty ice-blue eyes.

Her hat was on the ground. I picked it up and handed it to her.

"Thanks," she said, surprise still etched on her face.

After another beat, I added, "Are you one of my elves?"

She blinked a couple times after that and stepped out of my way. "Uh, yeah. I guess I am."

I took a seat in Santa's armchair. This chair was comfier than it looked.

"Sort of a last-minute thing... Didn't expect to," she went on.

Now I was looking up at her from my seat. She picked up a large tray of sugar cookies, like she was about to run off. But I didn't want her to leave yet.

"What's your name?" I asked.

"Oh," she said. Was it me or was she pretty nervous?

It had to be the suit. The costume was not like something you'd pick up at your local party store. It was the real deal. Between the large beard and the fake brows attached to my face, the special gloves, and the velvet suit that looked like it had been stitched by real elves, I couldn't even recognize myself in the mirror.

Best of all, I was really liking the anonymity.

"I'm Belle," she told me, her voice quiet.

I knew that, but I didn't want to let her know that. In fact, she couldn't know that.

I almost felt like a real-life Spiderman. I'd walked into the mall Nick St. James, then walked out of the bathroom as Saint Nicholas. No one knew it was me.

"Hi, Belle." I glanced down at the cookies she was holding. "Did you make those?"

"I did," she said, finally seeming to relax a little and smiling. She had a nice smile, the kind that made me forget who I was for a moment. "Would you like one?"

Sugar cookies were my favorite. I looked down and spotted a Santa Claus cookie, beard and all.

I picked it up and took a bite. "Mmm." I couldn't help myself. It was warm, buttery, and melted right in my mouth. I stared at Belle. "This is the best cookie I've ever had," I managed.

Her cheeks flushed pink. "Really?"

"Really," I said, taking another bite. "Hasn't anyone ever told you that before?"

She shook her head. "I just bake as a hobby."

"You should open your own store in town or something. These are incredible," I replied.

She blushed again. "I wish. Maybe someday."

Belle was a junior like me at Garland High. We were in all the same classes and were friendly, but we hung out in different friend groups. I knew her dad worked for the city doing road maintenance, but I didn't know much else about her.

After that, her mom appeared out of nowhere with a kid in tow. Belle scurried off with the rest of her cookies, and I focused on the little boy in front of me.

He looked excited but also very hesitant to come near me.

"Well, hello there!" I exclaimed, making my voice as deep and jolly as possible. "What's your name?"

He bit his lip and stared at the floor. "Ryan," he practically squeaked.

"Nice to meet you, Ryan," I replied. I noticed his Spiderman sneakers. Ryan was my kind of guy. "Do you like Spiderman?"

He nodded, a smile lighting up his face. "He's my favorite! My bed is Spiderman too!"

I grinned back. Yes, I was doing it. This was the part I'd been nervous about. "And do you have any Spiderman toys?" I asked.

He took a step closer, close enough to where I could put my arm around him. "Is it alright if I touch you?" I asked.

"Okay," he said. Then he told me about the Spiderman toys he wanted and the Spiderman books. And a ton of other stuff. Camera lights went off in front of us, but I hardly noticed them. I just listened to Ryan and nodded along when he asked me to please bring some toys for his baby sister too.

"Well, of course," I told him. He jumped up and down, and this time, we both smiled at the camera. The lady who had to be his mother stood near the stage holding a baby and beamed at me.

A second later, Belle was back, offering Ryan a cookie and leading him off the stage, his hand in hers.

My heart warmed, not believing I'd come full circle.

My mom had a picture at home on the mantle of me sitting on Garland Santa's lap, and now I was Santa.

I was no longer Nick, the star football player who was just seen for his popularity and what he could do on the field.

I was just a guy who could do some good in Garland.

A few weeks ago, my mom had said I'd make the perfect Santa. Had she made this happen? Maybe she had nominated me or something. Or maybe someone else had.

Before I could think too much about it, the next kid ran up to me.

This time, it was a girl, and she didn't seem nervous at all. She chatted my ear off, asking me questions about what the elves got to do at the North Pole, where I liked to go on vacation, and if it was okay if she stayed up and said hi to me on Christmas Eve.

"Ho, ho, ho!" I said, buying time to make up some answers. "Little boys and girls need their rest so they can open presents on Christmas morning."

I shot a glance at Belle, hoping she got the message that it was time to move on to the next kid in line.

She walked right over, saving my butt from fielding more questions I had no idea how to answer.

I'd had the biggest crush on her in the first grade. I still remembered being too chicken to give her the flower I'd found outside on the playground. Being this close to her now made me sweat a little, and it definitely wasn't just the heavy suit.

Now that we were working together, maybe this suit could give me something I never had back then. A little daring—and a real shot.

But would she ever go for me like this?

# 5
# BELLE

Santa Claus had never made butterflies appear in my tummy before.

Or left me completely breathless.

I never thought I'd daydream about finding myself back in Old St. Nick's arms either.

But here I was, doing just that as I mopped up coffee that one of the parents had spilled earlier.

I had no idea who was behind the thick white beard this year, but it definitely wasn't our math teacher. Or any other middle-aged man.

I moved the mop back and forth on the tile.

Something about his bright blue eyes and how he spoke told me he was young. And cute. Plus, definitely way more athletically built than any Santa I'd ever laid my eyes on.

I tore my gaze away from him, focusing on the spots I'd missed on the floor.

Was he a college student maybe? Someone I hadn't seen before or didn't really know? He didn't seem to be anyone I knew.

And he'd said my cookies were the best he'd ever tasted. I'd almost melted into a puddle when he'd said that.

I couldn't resist. Part of me already had the biggest crush on him, suit and all.

But more than anything, it was his eyes.

His kindness too. He made the perfect Santa, the way he talked to kid after kid after kid and still smiled and hung on to every word.

No one ever knew Santa's real identity, though. It was part of the magic, so I knew it was impossible for me to even try to snoop and find out.

You just didn't do that. It was like telling a kindergartener that Santa Claus wasn't real. It was a big no-no.

A little boy ran past, almost knocking me over. What was it about malls and kids just running wild?

"Careful!" I called after him. Thankfully, he'd just missed the wet spot.

I glanced at my phone with a sigh.

I was counting down the minutes until it was time to go home. The sooner I had a cup of hot chocolate in my hands, maybe a croissant too, the better.

My feet hurt and this costume itched. When it came to the festivities, I much preferred baking cookies to being an elf.

Santa had to be hot in his suit too. That suit looked thick enough to keep you warm at the North Pole. It had to be torture anywhere else.

Thirty minutes later, Santa hugged the last kid goodbye.

This part of the mall was pretty empty now. My stomach growled for food.

Santa Claus finally stood up from his chair, and my mom walked over to him.

I couldn't hear what they were saying, but I was sure he'd have to be back again soon. Handsome Santa and his elves would be invited to several more events like today.

Mom came over to me next. "Oh, honey, thank you so much. I owe you big time. I've gotta say, though, you are the cutest elf I've ever seen."

"Mom!" I whisper-whined. She said that way too loud, especially with Handsome Santa still being within earshot.

She glanced around sheepishly. "Sorry, sweetie." She checked her watch. "Fifteen more minutes to clean up, then hot chocolate is on me, okay?"

I perked up. "You read my mind."

Before she could scamper off, she looked at me one more time. "Can I count on you as one of my elves the rest of this week?"

I groaned, but she looked like she was ready to beg if necessary. "Fine," I replied. "But you really, really owe me."

I couldn't help it. I glanced past her at St. Nick, who was helping the elves carry the registration table to the back.

Mom caught me looking. "There's something about him, right?"

*There sure is*, I thought.

She finally left, and I put my mop and bucket away.

When I came back out, back in my own clothes, just about everyone was gone. No more elves. No more Santa.

But as I walked to Cocoa Corner with my mom in tow, my mind kept replaying that moment.

When I'd knocked straight into him and he'd caught me like it was nothing. His eyes had locked on mine for a split-second. Nothing like that had ever happened to me before.

I couldn't help but wonder: Was there any chance my Christmas wish could come true? My heart wanted to say yes, but my mind kept saying it had to be a fluke.

# 6
# NICK

My fish, Goldie, nibbled at his food flakes inside his glass bowl. I took a look at the small container. "I don't know what they put in this stuff, Goldie, but you're definitely in the running for the world record for longest living goldfish."

I'd had Goldie around for almost as long as I could remember. He'd been my birthday present the year after Dad had died, which meant Goldie had to be about a hundred years old in fish years by now, but he seemed as in tip-top shape as ever.

Maybe he had some of that Garland magic in him.

I walked into the kitchen, finding Mom sitting at the table with some food. I bent down to give her a hug. She hadn't asked too much about where I'd been recently. She kept pretty busy herself, and she knew I always picked up odd jobs here and there. I wasn't the kind to be out getting into trouble.

Little did she know the part-time job I'd landed this year.

"Doing okay, hon?" she asked. She had my favorite meal going on the stove. Her special homemade chili. At this rate, I'd be filling out that Santa suit in all the worst ways.

I rubbed my hands together. "I am now. We still on for movie night tomorrow?"

She smiled and reached up to kiss me on the cheek. "Wouldn't miss it for the world."

About once a month, we set aside a little money to go to A Wonderful Film, the movie theater in town. That place had to be a hundred years old, in the best way. They always played Christmas movies and showed classics for a dollar on Tuesdays. We'd go there then to Scrooge's for a greasy burger and fries afterward.

A lot of guys hated the idea of spending time with their mom like that, but we'd always been close, and she was pretty laid-back too.

I watched her carefully stir the big pot of chili.

When did those lines appear on her forehead? She worked way too hard. I made a mental note to get her a gift card to the spa or something. This Santa gig had to pay good money, right? And she never did anything nice for herself. There were always bills to pay.

Thinking about the perfect present for her, I bundled up, pulled on my snow boots, and grabbed the shovel from the garage. Then I headed outside. It had snowed several inches overnight, which meant there was work to do.

I took a breath of the freezing cold air. Most people hated being out in this weather, but I loved the quiet and the physical work. Not to mention I always enjoyed the view of Garland when it looked just like a winter wonderland.

A while later, I couldn't even feel the cold anymore. That was shoveling driveways for ya. I'd finished our driveway so Mom could head to work, but I was halfway through with Mr. and Mrs. Bowman's too. Old Mr. Bowman had taken a fall last winter, and ever since then, I tried to help out wherever I could, especially with yard work and things like that.

It was just the right thing to do. I didn't have many memories with Dad, but if he'd been around long enough to teach me anything, it was to help where you could.

"Hey, Nick!" It was Chad, one of the guys from the football team. He was on his bike.

I waved at him. I hadn't seen him since school had let out for winter break. "Hey, man!" I shouted. "What are you up to?"

He came to a stop a few feet away from me. "Headed to the ice-skating rink with some people from school."

I nodded. "Cool."

"You should come. We texted the Reindeer group chat," he said.

"Oh, sorry, I've barely looked at my phone all morning."

"That's too bad. Mindy and the rest of the cheerleaders are gonna be there."

"Oh really?" He had the biggest crush on Mindy, the captain.

"Maybe she'll finally go with me to Mistletoe Hill, you know what I mean?" he cracked.

I kind of smiled, but wished I could get back to my music and snow shoveling.

Chad was alright most of the time, but now that we were high school juniors on the football team, he and a lot of the guys just saw the cheerleaders as another notch on their belt. The more girls you took to Mistletoe Hill, the more the rest of the team looked up to you.

It was not my jam at all, but because I was on the football team like them, they thought I was all over that too.

"Well, I'll see you later then," he said.

"See you later," I said, putting my earbuds back in.

As I kept working, I couldn't help but think about the one girl who had caught my attention in that way.

It was probably a combination of the elf skirt she wore, her homemade cookies, and her sweet smile. Why had we never really talked before?

It was too bad, now that we were gonna be working together, because I couldn't even tell her who I really was.

That was what I'd agreed to when I put on the suit. She could never know who I was.

But that didn't mean I didn't want to spend time with her. Or wouldn't.

## 7
## BELLE

*A* couple of days later, I baked another big batch of cookies. This time, chocolate chip with and without pecans.

When baking was your favorite pastime and you dreamed of having your own bakery in town one day, you quickly ended up with four dozen cookies taking up all of the counter space in just one afternoon. So once they cooled, I wrapped them all up in tiny little plastic bags and packed them into a giant holiday basket.

I still had a couple hours before my shift as an elf at the mall. I'd have plenty of time to distribute cookies. So I pulled on my hat, mittens, and scarf and made my way into town.

Jingles was the famous chocolate shop in town.

We also had Candy Cane Co., where you could stand at the window and watch Neve Cole make candy canes from scratch. And we even had Cocoa Corner, possibly my favorite, where you could get the best hot chocolate and coffee in town.

But there was no bakery. Garland needed a bakery with the best cookies, scones, and muffins in town. Maybe one day that dream would come true. In a few more years perhaps I'd muster up the courage to make that wish upon the Christmas star. For now, I'd perfect my baking as much as I could and keep spreading holiday cheer via cookies.

I walked into Santa's Bag first. It was a souvenir store that had been running for almost a century. Old Mrs. Curran stood behind the register. Their tiny store had everything from the most unique, handcrafted tree ornaments to holiday mugs and tiny holiday trinkets.

Mrs. Curran always lit up when she saw me. I came by every year to drop off some cookies.

"Good afternoon!" I said. "I brought cookies."

"Belle," she replied with her usual smile. Her hazel eyes gleamed from behind her glasses. She wore a thick blue knit sweater with yellow stars all over it. "You're one of my favorite reasons for the season," she quipped.

Smiling at her, I took out several bags of cookies from my basket. "For you and Mr. Curran."

"Thank you, dear." She held up a cookie. "These are my favorite."

That's why I'd baked chocolate chip pecan this morning. Especially for her. She knew about my secret hopes to open a bakery one day, and she was my biggest cheerleader. "I hope you enjoy them."

"Oh, I definitely will. Won't be long now before you're running that bakery of yours."

I couldn't help but grin. "I hope you're right, Mrs. Curran."

Mr. Curran appeared from behind a shelf and joined her behind the counter. "She's never wrong," he chimed in. "Number one secret for a long and happy marriage," he whispered to me.

Mrs. Curran laughed, playfully hitting him on the shoulder.

I said goodbye and headed off to my next stop.

I went by the Snowed Inn and dropped off some cookies at the front desk for their guests. Mr. Atwood saw me with my basket on the way back out. "Are those your homemade cookies?" he asked.

"Yes, sir," I replied.

He nodded. "Must make for a fun hobby, especially for a young girl like yourself. I'm sure you'll be baking cookies for your own family soon enough."

He left before I could say another word.

As I walked out the front doors and down the steps, I couldn't help but feel a little irked. Every year, I got at least one comment like that. They meant well, but it annoyed me anyway. To me, baking was so much more than just a hobby. It felt like a calling. This was the one thing I was good at in a world where I felt invisible all the time. Especially to boys.

I went by Santa's Elves and The Nutcracker, a home decor store, next trying to get my mind off of the hobby comment. Santa's Elves housed a food pantry and ran all of Garland's local charity work. They made sure Christmas was magical for every family in Garland. My parents sponsored this place every year. Meanwhile, The Nutcracker was run by another one of my favorite old ladies, Ms. Merriweather.

By the time I made it to Cider Center and the

Garland Mall and transformed into one of Santa's elves in a too-small bathroom, I'd been walking around for a while.

*Maybe I should've thought of that before*, I thought to myself.

When I walked out in my costume, Santa was already there, saying hi and talking to people.

I hadn't seen him when I'd first arrived, but it made sense that whoever was behind the suit wouldn't get ready here.

I'd saved a few cookies especially for him, since he'd liked them so much last time.

My stomach swirled with nerves just at the thought of going up to him, but I grabbed a bag of chocolate chip cookies and walked his way to say hi.

"Belle," he said. "Hi."

He knew my name? I quickly racked my mind, trying to remember if I'd told him my name.

"Hi," I replied, walking up to him. We stood near the winter wonderland backdrop where we'd be working together for the next several hours.

"More cookies?" he asked. Once again, the only part of his face I could really see were his sparkling blue eyes. Everything else was hidden by his disguise, and part of me ached to see the rest of his face.

I nodded and handed him the bag of cookies. "For you," I told him. "Chocolate chip this time."

His white eyebrows raised a little in surprise. "Really? How thoughtful of you. Thank you."

My face felt hot, and I clasped my hands nervously. "You're welcome. Baking is one of my favorite things to do."

"That's impressive," he said.

I felt my face turning hot again. Before I could say anything, one of the elves came and grabbed him, whisking him away.

He was an important guy. Too important to stand around talking to me, that's for sure.

Later, when our shift was finally over and I was about ready to collapse, he came up to me again. The cookies I'd given him earlier were in his hand.

"You did a great job again today," I told him. "You're so good with the kids."

His eyes crinkled. "Thanks," he said. "I'm starting to think maybe I should study to be a teacher or something."

*A clue*, I thought. So he hadn't finished college yet. That confirmed why he seemed so young.

"You totally should," I replied.

"Anyway, I just wanted to say thanks again for these," he said, holding up the cookies.

"You're welcome," I said, getting ready to say goodbye and leave. He was just being polite. No one like him had ever acted interested in me before.

"Has anyone ever told you that you should be a professional baker?" he asked.

My heart lifted at the compliment, but I had to tell him the truth. "Most people think it's just a hobby, I guess," I said with a shrug.

His brows knitted together. "A hobby? That's like saying Lebron James has a hobby of playing basketball. Or that Lionel Messi has a hobby of playing soccer."

I smiled. "I don't know who that is, but I'll take your word for it."

He pulled a cookie out of the bag and took a bite. "Mm, definitely not a hobby."

My smile grew wider. Were those butterflies in my stomach again? Couldn't be. I tried to ignore them.

"I was going to ask you… How do you make all the different shapes? I always wondered how people did that."

Was he really asking me to nerd out right now?

"Well, I always shape mine by hand. But there's actually a special machine that professional bakers use to shape cookies faster and easier. It's a whole thing," I said, making myself not go on and on about it.

"Really?" he asked, taking another bite.

"Really," I said. "I'd love to have one, but they're expensive. Maybe next year."

His eyes twinkled again. "Maybe you should ask Santa to bring you one then," he said. "I hear you can write him a letter asking for such things."

I smiled. "You don't say?"

He held up a finger. "But not if you end up on the naughty list, of course."

My cheeks were starting to hurt from smiling so much. "Uh oh, I might be in trouble then."

We said our goodbyes, and I started making my way home, smiling like a complete doofus. My heart still pounding at the way he looked at me.

Uh oh.

I was falling in love with a guy… but I had no idea who he was.

## 8
## NICK

It took some hunting and searching around town, but a couple days later, I found it.

I found the machine Belle has been wanting. According to Ms. Merriweather at The Nutcracker, it was called a dough sheeter machine. And she happened to have one in stock. Just one. Gently used but in great condition.

And she'd given me a great deal on it.

"Are you sure?" I'd asked, holding the small but heavy cookie-shaping machine in my hands.

She'd patted my shoulder. "Least I can do after you fixed Bessie last year."

Bessie was her trusty old van, and it had to be older than me. The radiator had gone out last fall, and I'd picked up enough about cars in my auto shop class to replace it for her.

"Thanks, Ms. Merriweather," I told her gratefully. I had googled this thing, and a new one cost a pretty penny.

She walked me to the front and helped me wrap it up. How she knew it was a gift I didn't know, but that was Ms. Merriweather for ya. She just knew things sometimes.

As I walked out of The Nutcracker, I held the package gingerly under my arm. I hoped Belle liked it.

The sound of singing voices reached me from across the street. Which made sense since it looked like Garland's favorite group of carolers were on their usual tour around town, singing Christmas songs. The small but mighty group of old ladies stood in front of Jingles, the Garland chocolate shop. Some people called them the Carol Karens. They were the kind of women who knew (and spread) the town's juiciest gossip.

*Better head the other way*, I thought to myself.

I couldn't risk any questions.

Not today.

I also wasn't sure how good I was at keeping secrets. I'd never had to keep a secret like the one I had this year. Back home, my Santa suit lay hidden on the very top shelf of my closet, where I knew Mom couldn't reach.

And now I had a gift for the cute elf I'd made friends with at the mall.

Maybe wanted to be more than friends with, if I was being completely honest.

There was just something about Belle that was special. That much I knew.

Hopefully, she liked my gift.

Or rather, Santa's gift.

The next day, I got to the mall early and changed in the southeast bathrooms as usual. They had a family bathroom that hardly anyone ever used because it was so far from the food court and everything else.

Then I made my way down to the big area near the food court with the nice water fountain and the place where kids lined up to meet Santa.

Still crazy to think that guy was me.

There was a big Christmas tree inside the mall, along with the giant tree at Cider Center outside. It wasn't too far from where I sat and took photos.

I carefully set down the wrapped gift under the tree. This was definitely a first for me, so I was nervous, but I wasn't going to chicken out now.

About fifteen minutes later, I sat in my chair when Belle walked on set and gave me a wave and smile.

I smiled and waved back. She probably couldn't see my smile under this thick white beard. Then again, it might also hide the way I looked at her.

After countless kids—some smiling, some crying—we were finished for the day, and everyone was tired.

And I was more nervous than ever about Belle's gift.

As she walked over to me, I couldn't help but wonder: Was it me or did she seem a little nervous too?

That's when she pulled out a bag of cookies from behind her back. "Snickerdoodles this time. Thought you might like some."

I couldn't believe it. "If they're anything like your other cookies, I'm sure they'll be amazing."

A familiar rosy hue came over her cheeks, and I took the cookies from her. My gloved hands touched hers, and I wished, in that moment, I could actually take her hand in mine.

Our eyes locked for a second, and I forgot who I was.

Then I saw the Christmas tree behind her and

remembered her gift. It sat among the dozen or so fake ones.

I nodded toward the tree. "I think there's something for you under that tree," I said.

I immediately wished I could've gone about it in a less lame way.

She turned around, then glanced back at me. "Something for me?"

We walked over there together. Just about everyone else had already left or had gone off to grab some food from the food court, so it was mostly just us.

Belle saw the package that stood out from the rest and picked it up. She looked up at me. "Who is this from?"

"Santa Claus, who else?" I teased. "Looks like you made it on the nice list this year."

She glanced down at the gift, a huge smile on her face.

"Open it," I said, unable to help myself.

I held the box for her, and she undid the bow and took off the lid.

She gasped. "You didn't!"

I noticed how close she was standing to me.

"Where'd you find it?" she asked.

I shrugged. "Special order to the North Pole."

She laughed, then looked back down at the machine. "Wow, I can't wait to use it."

A beat passed, then she said, "Thank you. I don't know what else to say."

I saw tears brim in her eyes.

Uh oh. I knew girls cried when they were happy sometimes. Were these happy tears? I hoped so. Pretty sure they were.

"Hey," I said as she put the lid back on the box. I wasn't ready for us to part ways just yet. "You want to go get a coffee with me?" I paused. "Well, with Santa Claus?"

9
BELLE

*I* couldn't believe it.

I was really going to have coffee with...

With Santa Claus?

No, definitely not Santa Claus.

Santa was not a hot young guy with piercing but friendly blue eyes. And I could see enough of his fit figure underneath that big suit to know whoever was behind the disguise was absolutely FINE.

I changed out of my elf suit, feeling self-conscious. No guy had ever paid me any attention before—especially not one as hot as him.

Could I have joined him in costume? Yes. Was I

about to go out as an elf in public with a hot Santa to impress? Absolutely not.

Not when I had my pretty brown sweater and best pair of blue jeans waiting for me in the back room. Those jeans always made my butt look good, and today, I needed all the help I could get.

I checked myself in the mirror. Good thing I was having a good hair day too.

I dug into my bag. All I was missing was... found it. Some strawberry lip gloss.

When I stepped back out, Santa was there. "No elf costume?"

I shook my head. "Definitely no elf costume."

He kind of glanced down at his suit. "Lucky you."

Santa Claus and I headed to Cocoa Corner together.

That was not on my bingo board for the year, that's for sure.

"This thing does keep me pretty warm, though," he said as we walked.

I touched his sleeve. "I bet."

We got tons of curious looks, and plenty of kids stopped Santa along the way for a selfie.

Luckily, Cocoa Corner was pretty much empty when we got there.

Jack stood behind the counter and did a doubletake when we approached the register. He looked like he'd seen pigs flying out his window. Clearly, Santa had never walked in here.

"Special friend there, Belle?" he asked.

We reached him. "Something like that," I said, looking at ol' St. Nick next to me.

He waved and said, "Ho, ho, ho," in his Santa voice. He was very good at it, like he'd been practicing for years.

Nick chuckled. "Well, what can we get you guys?"

"I'll take my usual, please," I told him, adjusting my bag on my shoulder.

"One large hot chocolate and one apple cinnamon bagel. Got it." He looked at Santa.

"Uh, same."

A minute later, we sat in the booth at the corner with our drinks and toasted bagels slathered in cream cheese.

Santa had his back to the window like he didn't want to get distracted by all the people gawking as they walked by—although he kind of stood out anyway.

Meanwhile, I tried not to let my nerves get the

best of me. I had no idea how I'd ended up becoming friends with Santa Claus.

Much less how I'd ended up with a huge crush on him.

Trying to push that aside, I took a sip of my hot chocolate. "So…" I started, unsure of what I should ask or not.

"So…" he replied, probably wondering the same thing.

"What topics should I avoid?" I tried.

He shrugged. "My name, I guess." He pondered for a second. "And anything that would give away who I am."

"Shouldn't be too hard," I retorted.

He smiled. "Try being in my shoes."

"What is it like being in those shoes?" I asked, slowly stirring the dissolving marshmallows around my drink.

He stared down at his hot chocolate for a second. "Pretty good, actually," he replied. "It's nice not being… who I usually am."

I took another sip. "Really?"

"I guess people are used to seeing me a certain way, and sometimes, it just feels like a mismatch with who I want to be, you know?"

I nodded again. "That makes sense. High school

isn't always easy." Although, if he was as good looking as I suspected, he was probably one of the popular kids.

"Yea—" he began. "I mean, I can neither confirm nor deny that."

"What's your favorite color?" I asked. That had to be a safe question.

"Blue," he answered. "Typical, huh?"

"Kind of," I said, clearly not getting a clue about who he was.

"What about you?" he asked. He took a bite of his bagel.

"Lilac," I replied. My room was lilac, and I always gravitated toward the color for phone cases and notebooks and the like.

Silence fell between us while I tried to come up with a question to narrow down who he was without being too obvious. "So, what do you like to do for fun? Do you play sports or anything?" I asked.

He thought about it for a second. "I do things for fun," he said finally.

That made me think he definitely did extracurriculars at school. And with his build, I bet he had to be some sort of jock. A wrestler maybe?

We had a relatively small school, but still plenty

of jocks. Most of whom pretended I didn't exist, especially around school dance times and Valentine's Day. But I tried not to think about that or let my doubts get in my way. Santa was being so nice I didn't want my insecurities to ruin anything.

After that, we ended up talking more about our past and future than the present. Much safer topics of conversation.

"Best Christmas present you ever got?" I asked.

He paused, clearly thinking about it. "Probably… the beach vacation we went on last year. It was only a few days, but I'd never been to the beach. If I ever moved anywhere else, that's where I would go."

Garland citizens prided themselves on staying here for life, and rightly so.

"That would be my second choice too," I said.

"What about you?" he asked. "Favorite Christmas present?"

I smiled. "Easy." I held up the gift he'd given me earlier. "This."

"You're just being nice," he said.

I scoffed. "I'm not! No one's ever given me something like this before. It was very thoughtful."

There was a beat of silence after that. The kind where it was hard to look at each other.

His hand covered mine for a second, and my breath hitched.

Then his hand was back on his mug.

I couldn't believe he had really reached over to touch my hand.

I also couldn't believe what a cool person he was.

And it was driving me crazy not knowing who he really was.

All this time, and we'd never become friends until now?

We finished our hot chocolates and kept talking. This time about what we wanted to do after high school or college.

"I can totally see you opening up a bakery," he said.

"Thanks. You'll get free cookies for life for being my first investor," I teased.

He gave a "Yes!" and made a motion like he'd gotten the high score.

I smiled. "What about you?"

"I don't know yet. I like talking to and helping people." He shrugged. "If wearing this suit has taught me anything, it's that."

Aw, who was this guy? He was not like any jock I'd ever met.

"Maybe you'll be the next mayor of Garland," I quipped.

He grinned. "Maybe," but he sounded sarcastic. "I don't know if I'd want to be in the spotlight, though."

He looked like he wanted to go on, but he didn't.

That made me think he was familiar with being in the spotlight, but I didn't ask.

Instead, we got up. He had somewhere he had to be, and I had to get home.

He walked me a couple of blocks before turning toward Tinsel Terrace.

With my gift in hand, I walked the rest of the way home, grinning like a complete doofus.

## 10
## NICK

The next time I saw Belle, I had a proposal for her.

It was for a good cause, but also, I'd get to spend more time with her.

If she was agreeable.

"You know Santa's Elves off of Elm?" I asked.

We'd completed another Saturday of photos and listening to lots and lots of Christmas wishes. Which meant I was all geared up in my suit. These days, it felt like I spent a lot of time in this suit.

Belle nodded. She was still in her elf suit. "Yeah. My mom is good friends with Ms. Merriweather."

"Well," I began. I almost let it slip that I volunteered there a lot. "What do you think about baking some cookies for the families in need this year?"

Her eyes lit up. "I could put your gift to good use!"

I smiled. Also a big pro, aside from hanging out with her again. "Exactly."

"Aw," she said. "What a sweet idea. It would make me really happy knowing that my cookies might bring some smiles to kids who had a tough year."

I wished I could've told her about how I volunteered there every week, invited her to come along even.

Maybe someday.

Today, I'd settle for a couple of hours with her.

We met at Santa's Elves the next day. We were both off work, but since I couldn't let her see who I really was, I was stuck in my suit again.

Santa's Elves was officially closed, but I knew where Ms. Merriweather hid the spare key to the back door.

I dug it out from under an inconspicuous rock near the dumpster.

Belle didn't look so sure. She was holding on to a large wagon full of baking supplies and the machine I'd gifted her. "Are you sure this is okay?"

## 11
## NICK

The first time I put on this suit, it was great. Getting to be anonymous. Getting to be someone other than Nick St. James for once.

The guy everyone had figured out.

But now that I'd gotten close to Belle, the one thing I craved was leaving this suit behind so she could get to know the real me.

Even if I could, though, wouldn't that complicate things?

I carefully put on my fake white eyebrows and placed the beard over my face.

I had no idea.

What if she didn't like Nick St. James like she liked the guy behind this suit?

I finished my sugar cookie. "You really do make the best cookies. You've got real talent, Belle."

She blushed a little but didn't look away. "Thank you."

The way she said it made me think that no one ever told her that. Well, I'd never let her forget it.

It wasn't long before we had a huge batch of cookies cooling on the counters.

Belle sat on one of the stools, and I sat on another one a couple feet away. "This was a lot of fun."

I gave her a small smile from behind my beard. "I had a blast."

We both glanced around. "It's gonna suck to clean all of this up, though," I added.

There was flour everywhere.

"I'll wipe everything down if you take mopping duty," she said.

"Deal," I replied.

Neither of us got up.

She looked as worn out as me.

"In two more minutes," I said.

Our reward for the hour it took to get the kitchen back to spic and span was getting to sample the cooled treats. We had a mix of perfectly shaped sugar cookies and chocolate chip cookies on the cooling rack.

Belle took a bite of her cookie. I noticed she could hardly stop admiring all of them. "I think these are the best cookies I've ever made. They look perfect."

They sure did.

Belle was laughing. "Earth to Santa, Earth to Santa."

Oh man, had she caught me daydreaming?

I grabbed some flour and threw it at her.

She screamed, trying to dodge it, but it covered her hair.

"Hey, now you look like Mrs. Claus," I joked.

"You're the worst!" she said, but she was smiling as she tossed some back at me.

Pretty soon, we were both covered.

I looked down at my suit. "I doubt I can just throw this thing in the wash when I get home."

She patted my shoulder hard, trying to brush the flour away. "Dry clean only, I bet."

My hand came up and touched her hair.

I think we both realized at the same time just how close we were.

Her eyes locked on mine.

I knew what I wanted to do next.

I wondered if she wanted the same thing.

I glanced down at her lips, rosy and full as ever.

Then the oven timer went off, and we both jumped. A second later, we were laughing. She hung onto my arm for a moment before going over to the oven.

"Right in here," I said, leading the way.

Belle got to work, preheating the giant oven and setting out all her ingredients.

"You really make these from scratch?" I asked.

She almost looked offended. "Would there be any other way?"

I rubbed my hands together. "Will you show me your secret recipe?"

She grinned. "Maybe. If I can trust you with it, that is."

I feigned an offended gasp. "If you can trust me? I'm Santa Claus. If you can't trust me, who can you trust?"

She laughed and kept measuring flour.

Whenever she asked me to hand her stuff, I obliged. This was clearly her zone of genius, and it only made me like her even more.

When she was busy sifting flour and pouring chocolate chips, I couldn't help but notice how soft her hair looked and think about bringing my lips to hers.

Not that that would even be possible with this giant beard I was wearing.

Next thing I knew, there was flour on my face. "Hey!" I cried out.

I opened the door and held it open. "I'm sure."

Between my belly and her wagon, it turned into a bit of an ordeal to get us and the wagon through the doorway. I shifted, trying to make room, but ended up chest to chest with her.

My breathing sped as I realized just how close we were, catching the scent of her perfume and seeing her cheeks flush as she looked up at me. I swallowed hard and moved to the side, getting through the door so she could follow.

The door finally closed behind us. It was nice and toasty inside, but nothing compared to the heat spreading in my chest.

Belle laughed breathily. "Are you sure you don't want to change out of that costume into something more suitable for cooking?"

I shook my head. "Wish I could, but no. You know how sacred this job is."

"I do," she replied.

We made our way to the kitchen. Luckily, this place had one and I wouldn't need to show up at Belle's house like this. Talk about an awkward conversation with her parents.

It also had a storeroom with all kinds of stuff, donations mostly. We passed it on the way to the kitchen.

But I didn't want to think about that now.

I pulled on my boots, already running late to meet her.

As I headed out the front door, I narrowly avoided running into Mom.

"Nick! Give me a hug before you leave. I won't see you until tonight. Where did you say you were going after work?"

Already halfway down the hallway, there was no way I was going to be able to hide in time.

Thankfully, her cell phone rang at just the right moment. She turned around to go back and grab it. I heard her go into the kitchen, taking the call that had come in.

I took my chance and made a run for it.

Before I closed the back door behind me, I shouted a quick, "Bye, Mom! I'll text you later. Love you!"

I dashed into the tree line just in case she had followed me, but it looked like I was in the clear.

This was a well-known path for me now. It would lead me out near Rudolph's place. He was an odd fella, famous for his sleigh rides around town. And the perfect way for me to sneak into town.

By the time I made it to Santa's Elves, Belle was already there.

She smiled when she saw me enter one of the large back rooms. "Hey, you. Did the reindeer hit traffic?" she teased.

I grinned at her joke. "Something like that."

I wished this job came with a sweet ride, and I almost wondered out loud where I could submit that sort of feedback.

Clearly, Belle had already gotten a head start.

There were supplies at the ready and presents all around the room, from bright blue and pink bikes to pajamas, books, and all sorts of toys.

"Ms. Merriweather said she'll be back later. She had to make a run to the bank and a couple of other places and told me to lock up if we finished before she got back," Belle said.

I nodded. "Sounds like a plan."

We got to work wrapping presents. Pretty quickly, I realized I was nowhere near as good as Belle at wrapping.

She tried not to laugh at the oddly shaped gift in my hands.

"I know," I responded. "It looks like a first grader wrapped it."

She opened her mouth, closed it, then said, "I didn't say that."

She scooted closer to me and gave me some lessons.

I loved being this close to her, even if I didn't love being in this suit right then and there. It sure didn't make it easy to move around.

"Okay, I think I got it," I said.

I gave it another try, this time with a puzzle. I held it up for Belle's approval.

She nodded. "Better. Definitely better."

I stuck to the easy stuff, anything that was square or rectangular in nature. And she took care of all the advanced stuff, like soccer balls and dinosaurs.

"You're a whiz at this," I pointed out.

She grinned. "Lots of practice."

Her phone buzzed, and she checked it, setting down her scissors to text someone back. She glanced up at me when she was done. "My friend Holly."

I knew Holly. Or at least I knew who she was.

"Hanging out with them this week?" I asked, picking up another board game.

She shook her head. "We've all been pretty

busy. Probably not until Christmas Eve or after. What about you and your friends?"

"Also pretty busy," I replied, although I had to be the busiest one this year. "I'm sure we'll hang out for New Year's. Should be fun."

"Maybe by then, I'll get to see you without that beard," she teased.

I couldn't help but smile. "Maybe." There was always a big New Year's Eve party at somebody's house. The thought of inviting Belle and kissing her as we rang in the new year... I couldn't think of anything better.

She finished wrapping a big art set. I watched her wrap and cut the tape just right, then put together a bow. Instead of grabbing one of the bows you just stuck on there, though, she pulled out a spool of Christmas ribbon. Mesmerized, I watched her maneuver the ribbon, wrap it round and round, snip a little here, snip a little there... and boom. She'd made one of those big fancy bows. "You really are an elf!" I said.

That made her laugh, which made me grin like a fool.

"It's not that hard, I promise." She scooted toward me again and gave me the ribbon. "Here."

Her hands touched mine as she taught me how

to wind up the ribbon and do the rest, but I was already lost. The only thing I could remotely pay attention to was her.

Her lips were perfect, and all I wanted to know was what they tasted like.

Probably vanilla like her perfume.

Just like that, she seemed to notice that I wasn't paying attention at all.

Her eyes locked on mine, and just as I was tugging away my beard to finally kiss her, we heard Ms. Merriweather shout from the front.

"Belle? I'm back!" she called.

We pulled apart; the magic gone.

## 12
## BELLE

The next day at Cider Center was especially busy. With Christmas right around the corner, everyone and their mama was out doing last-minute shopping.

Santa Claus had a line of families wanting their picture since eight o'clock this morning, and I hadn't had a minute to stop and take a break since then.

There were babies, toddlers, and kids of all ages running around, screaming and itching to get their turn with Santa.

I tried to keep them occupied with songs and free snacks while they waited in line, but the mall was still chaos.

Halfway through my shift, I switched places

with one of the other elves, and I helped lead kids away from Santa once their turn was done.

At one point, I even saw Carolynn shopping at the mall, but all I had time for was a quick wave before chasing after a runaway preschooler.

After I finally helped his mom get ahold of him, I gave Santa a glance. He gave me a knowing look from where he sat.

Meanwhile, the next child had both of us tearing up. A sweet little girl with braids who told Santa she didn't want anything for Christmas this year. She just wanted her daddy to be happy again because ever since Grandpa had passed away to heaven, he'd been really, really sad.

I held her hand and looked toward Santa, but he kept his gaze on her face and his gloved hand on her shoulder. "I see." There was a pause, and I wondered if he knew what to say. Just as I was about to interrupt and change the subject to something happier, he went on. "It's not easy when someone you love passes away. Your daddy is sad because he loves your grandpa very much."

"But when will he stop being sad?" she asked, curious.

Santa exhaled. "Well, he might be sad any time he thinks about Grandpa and all the fun memories.

But the important thing is to remember Grandpa together and talk about all the fun times. That'll help your daddy feel better."

Goosebumps ran down my arms. I'd never heard him talk about anything like this before. It sounded like he was talking from a deeply personal experience.

He glanced at me, and I gave him a small smile. He turned back to Leila, the little girl. "Your daddy is going to be alright. And I'm sure he wants you to have a beautiful Christmas. Now tell me, how can I help make it special?"

She finally told him about the doll she wanted and ask if he could please bring one for her little sister too.

"You got it, Leila," he said with a grin. She gave him a big hug, and he squeezed her in return. Then she ran right to her parents, who were holding her baby sister. The mom mouthed *thank you,* and I swore I saw the dad blinking back tears before they all walked away.

Before the next kid came up, I asked Santa, "How'd you know what to say?"

He shrugged. "My dad died when I was little. I guess I know what it's like to lose someone."

Before I could say anything else, a little boy hopped up on his lap, going right into his wish list.

During the final leg of our shift, my mom found us. There was a rare lull, so she gave us a quick five-minute break. A couple of the other elves ran to the restroom. Meanwhile, all I wanted to do was sit.

Mom went up to Santa, offering him an iced coffee. "You're the best Santa we've had in a long time!" she told him.

Santa grinned and took the coffee. "Thank you, Mrs. Finch. It's been an honor."

After that, she took off again, clipboard in hand. As she went to talk to her janitorial team, I walked up to Santa.

"You're a natural," I told him, deciding not to bring up what he'd said earlier. "The kids love you."

He glanced around. "Is that why we're so busy?"

I looked at the long line. "Probably." Then I turned my gaze on him again. "You've got the best job too, sitting down all day. You know how many four-year-olds I've chased down today? I mean, what are their parents giving them before coming here? A whole gallon of hot chocolate?"

Santa laughed. "Actually, you're probably not far off."

There were holiday treats galore at the mall this time of year.

"You know," Santa went on, "you're welcome to sit on my lap if you want." His blue eyes sparkled mischievously as he patted his thigh.

I immediately felt my face turn hot, and I nudged him playfully. "I don't think Mrs. Claus would appreciate that," I joked. "It would really get the rumors going at the North Pole, and we can't have that."

"Well, you know where to find me should you change your mind," he teased.

We got going again, and I went back to corralling crazy kids.

As I did, I couldn't help but think about what would happen once the Christmas season was over. Just a couple more days, and then I'd be out of this elf costume for good and so would Santa.

What would happen then? Would we be over too?

## 13
## NICK

I was just crazy about Belle. I couldn't get enough time with her.

So, after our shift, as we cleaned up for the day, I asked her out again.

I was counting down the days until I could get out of this Santa suit. I didn't know exactly what would happen with us, but I knew I wanted her to see and be with the real me.

Even if I was nervous about her finding out who I really was. Could that be a dealbreaker for her? We'd never run in the same circles before at school. And for some reason, it was always a big deal if jocks didn't go out with cheerleaders, like it was this unwritten rule that we were only supposed to date within our own circle.

I had no idea who had made up that rule, but I didn't want to follow it.

I pushed that out of my mind. For now, I just wanted to focus on Belle.

"So, what do you say?" I asked her. The mall was almost empty. "Come to the movies with me?"

She angled her head a bit as she swept around my chair. "Are you sure?"

I didn't miss a beat, helping move things out of the way. "Why wouldn't I be?"

She stopped and took in my suit. "Well, you have to stay in your suit, right?"

"Yeah," I replied. "Is that okay?" I wondered if it bothered her. It would definitely put us in the spotlight if we didn't find a way around it.

"It doesn't bother me," she said, going back to sweeping. "I was just wondering if it bothered you, having to be in it all the time."

I shrugged. "It's part of the job. No one can know who I am."

I held the dustpan for her as she finished up.

She gave me a small smile. "Okay," she said finally. "I'll go to the movies with you." She turned to leave, but then spun around to face me again. "It has to be a Christmas movie, though."

I grinned. "I wouldn't have it any other way."

Instead of going through the main part of town, we took the long way so we could avoid most of the foot traffic.

We also walked quickly because it was colder than ever. And windy. My hat almost blew off, but I grabbed it in time.

No one needed to see that Santa Claus had a full head of blonde hair.

We finally made it to A Wonderful Film. I went up to the counter and got us two tickets to *Home Alone*.

"This is definitely my favorite Christmas movie of all time," I said as we walked into the last theater at the end of the hall.

A few people sat chatting, eating their popcorn, and waiting for their movie to begin. They didn't notice Santa Claus come in with a cute girl behind him.

We went to one of the top rows and took a seat. The theater was already dark, and part of me wanted to take off my beard, at least. But I couldn't take that kind of risk. Not with Belle or anyone else.

"What's your favorite Christmas movie?" I asked her.

She munched on some popcorn, and I did the

same.

"Oh, definitely *The Grinch*. The one with Jim Carrey," she replied.

"That is the best one," I added. "Solid choice. If you had said anything else, I definitely would've judged you."

She smiled. "As long as you don't say that *Die Hard* is your favorite, I won't judge you."

I clutched at my chest. "It's not my favorite Christmas movie, but it's up there! *Die Hard* is definitely a Christmas movie."

I would die on this hill.

Belle rolled her eyes but smiled back. "I knew it. This friendship was doomed."

I laughed, and she did too, and then we both quieted down because the previews were starting.

"This is the best part," I whisper-shouted.

"Agreed!" she replied.

By the time we got to the part with the choir, I turned to look at Belle. This part always got me. She turned to me and smiled. Before I could think about it too much, I reached my hand over to find hers.

My gloves had come off earlier with the popcorn, so it almost felt like getting to share a small part of the real me. Her hand was soft. I gave it a squeeze, and we went back to the movie.

After it was over and Kevin got his family back and the credits were rolling, we sat there for a while just talking.

"Do you and your family have any fun traditions?" I asked her.

"Well, we always exchange books on Christmas Eve. Like a Secret Santa type thing. Then we read together, drink hot chocolate, and go to bed pretty early," she said. "After setting out cookies and milk for Santa, of course."

I nodded. "Of course. Very important."

She grinned. "What about you?"

"Well, we usually go to the Garland Express. My mom loves the sleigh rides. And then we walk through Tinsel Terrace. I like the lights. And then we go to Scrooge's," I finished. "It's kind of become a holiday tradition ever since I burned the turkey a couple years ago. And I think my mom likes not having to cook so much, especially since it's just the two of us."

"That sounds fun," she said. "Is it usually busy?"

I added, "No, actually. It's usually pretty quiet. And my mom likes to harass Henry. Really, I think she senses that he gets kind of lonely this time of year, so we always go and hang out with him."

Henry was the owner of Scrooge's, and he was kind of a real-life Scrooge. Older, kept to himself, didn't have much family around anymore. Mom said he reminded her of her dad.

"Henry always says he hates the holiday fuss, but I think you're right that he must just get a little lonely. That's sweet of you guys to check in on him."

"He also serves the best burgers and milkshakes in town," I said.

*Maybe soon, I could take her*, I thought.

## 14
## BELLE

As we walked out of the movie theater, I finally allowed myself to wonder what I'd been pushing to the back of my mind for a solid week now.

Was my Christmas wish really coming true?

It had been a big ask to be sure, but here I was, hand in hand with an amazing guy. Sure, I had no idea who he really was behind that suit, but my hand was wrapped in his and there were definitely sparks in the air.

I couldn't believe this was actually happening to me, even if I ached for my friends to experience the same thing.

Santa led me to a quiet place behind the movie theater where we could sit and take in the view of a good part of Garland. I could almost see the light of the star on the tree.

"I had a really nice time," I told him, wondering what his name was.

He sat down next to me. "Me too."

I shivered a little, and he scooted closer, wrapping his arm around me to warm me up.

Who needed a fireplace when you had a cute guy to keep you warm?

"Just a couple more days," he said, breaking the silence. "And then work at the mall will be done."

I looked at him. "I won't miss the chaos. Or that elf costume."

He smiled. "I will. I'll miss some other things too."

Butterflies filled my stomach as I wondered what he meant by that.

"Once you're out of that costume, how will I know who you are?" I asked.

He thought for a second, brushing a strand of hair out of my face. "I don't know. I guess I'll have to find you, huh?"

That would be weird, especially if I didn't know him in "real life." Or would it?

He went on. "Hopefully, you'll still like me when I'm out of this Santa suit."

I laughed. "It might be a dealbreaker; I don't know," I teased.

We grew silent again, both of us clearly with a lot on our minds.

"And then what? What happens after that?" I asked him quietly, kind of mesmerized.

"And then," he added, his voice also quiet, "I'm sure I'll do something I've been thinking about doing for a while now."

My breath hitched, completely transfixed by his bright blue eyes.

I hardly noticed, but snow began falling all around us, just like in the movies. Slow, soft, and white. It was like we were suddenly surrounded by the perfect Christmas backdrop.

Santa looked at my lips like he very badly wanted to do something, but also knew he couldn't.

Something like daring rose up in my chest, and before I could talk myself out of it, I looked at him and said, "I won't look." Then I closed my eyes. This was the only way.

Slowly, I felt for his beard with my hand, tugged it down, and leaned in, eyes still closed.

I felt his hand hold the side of my face, and a

second later, his mouth met mine, closing the gap between us.

Kissing him was better than anything I could've imagined. His nose pressed against my cheek, a little cold. My heart beat like a wild horse on the run. And he tasted like peppermint and Christmas.

After a minute, we pulled apart, and I felt him tugging his beard back on. Slowly, I blinked opened my eyes.

I had no idea who this boy was, but one thing was for sure. I'd never think about Christmas again without thinking of him.

## 15
## NICK

The next day, I was on cloud nine.

It felt like I was walking on water, and I couldn't stop thinking about Belle. Her soft lips. The way she closed her eyes and pulled my beard aside.

Wow.

I'd been shoveling snow for the past hour like it was nothing.

I couldn't wait to see her again, probably at work. I wondered if asking her out again would be too soon.

Or too risky.

At the end of the day, I wasn't supposed to let anyone know who I was. That was part of the deal.

But she was getting dangerously close to finding out.

Would I really stop her if she asked? I had no idea.

To be honest, I wanted her to know. I wanted her to see the real me, now that things were happening between us. It only felt right.

I kept shoveling, feeling sort of torn inside and hoping it was okay if I ended up breaking the rules. No one had to know but us.

Right?

A lone car drove past, and I gave one of the neighbors a wave.

I leaned against my shovel, taking a rest and replaying all of the times spent with Belle. How had I never realized how great she was?

A couple of people all bundled up walked past on the opposite sidewalk, with their dog leading the way.

It was cold out, and a fresh layer of snow from last night covered the ground.

Which was why I was out here shoveling again.

By the time I finished our driveway and got going on the neighbor's driveway, I was exhausted. Just as I was about to go back inside, I spotted a familiar figure coming my way.

Was that really…

Belle.

Getting ready to walk past me.

"Hey!" I said, then I realized there was no way she would know why I was talking to her. And that she'd recognize my voice. I cleared my throat and made myself speak a little deeper. "Hey, good morning!"

As she approached me on the sidewalk, her face went from surprise to confusion to polite friendliness.

She definitely didn't recognize me.

"Good morning," she called, coming to a stop near me.

I stood, leaning on my shovel. "Belle, right?" I asked, trying to strike up a conversation.

She nodded. "That's right. We're in the same grade, I think."

Belle looked like she was ready to make up an excuse and keep going on with her day.

I nodded at her basket. "Do you like to bake during the holidays?"

Now a smile came on her face. "Yeah, I guess it's my thing. I make tons of cookies every year."

"Cool," I replied. I indicated the piles of snow nearby. "I shovel a lot of snow."

"I bet it's a workout," she said, a little more friendly now.

I nodded again. "For sure. But it keeps me busy, and it helps out Mr. and Mrs. Bowman, who can't really do it anymore."

She glanced around. "You should start a business or something."

I grinned. "You're probably right. Although snowball fights are way more fun."

"Oh really?" she asked. "Aren't you a little old for snowball fights?"

She was teasing me in a way I was now familiar with, and I liked it.

It almost felt like our other conversations.

"You'd be surprised. I think they get way more fun when you're older." I held one finger. "For one, you can bring teams and strategy into it." I held up another finger. "And your aim is better." I held up a third finger. "And no one ends up crying. Usually."

That got a laugh out of her.

"My friend Kane actually has a whole business selling snowballs for snowball fights. You'd be surprised how popular it is."

She raised her brows. "Wow, really?" She paused. "I can't say that would be my go-to, but it sounds fun."

"What would be your go-to then?" I asked, shifting my weight on the shovel.

"Hot chocolate for one, inside," she said, shivering almost on cue. The tip of her nose was pink, and part of me wanted to brush her curls out of her face, but that was a no go. "And either a good book or a good movie. Or," she said, holding up her basket, "a couple of hours of baking with holiday music in the background."

"That sounds fun too," I said with a smile.

She smiled back. "It is. You should try it sometime."

"Maybe I will," I said.

I liked Belle. Every time I spoke to her, even now, it was like she didn't care about all the external stuff that everyone else in school cared about. She just saw me for me. She didn't treat me any different. And she was herself too.

For once, I couldn't wait until Christmas was over so I could be myself around her once and for all.

## 16
## BELLE

Nick St. James had never said one word to me before, and now here we were, having a whole conversation.

He was nice, with a nice smile to boot.

I just didn't understand how I'd ended up here, talking with him. He was the quarterback of the football team and probably one of the hottest guys at Garland High. But he'd always been the type to date cheerleaders and run in those circles.

His blonde hair peeked out from under his hat as he leaned on his snow shovel. He sure was built like a star football player, and he was handsome too.

"Drinking hot chocolate sure beats being out

here and shoveling snow," he said. "Where are you headed now?"

"Into town to drop these off to a few people I know," I said, showing him my basket. "I bake so many that they'd go to waste unless I gave some away."

"That's nice of you," he replied, and I realized how close we'd gotten. "I bet you end up on Santa's nice list every year."

His comment made me smile. "I do my best."

His eyes were an almost familiar striking blue, but something about them was different too. It just had to be a coincidence. Nick St. James couldn't be the guy I'd been spending so much time with this winter break. He had better things to do than play dress-up in a Santa suit.

There was something about the Santa I'd been hanging out with that was different. Something about his voice and demeanor that I surely would've recognized.

I had no idea why Nick St. James seemed interested in getting to know me, but it was odd.

And had butterflies going in my stomach.

Which quickly got replaced by a pit of guilt.

It felt weird and wrong to be talking to Nick St. James like this, especially after the sweet kiss and handholding I'd done with the boy behind the Santa suit the past few days.

I had no idea why Nick was talking to me all of a sudden. Maybe he was in between girlfriends, or maybe it was a dumb bet with his friends that he should talk to the next girl who came down the sidewalk.

I didn't really know him that well, so I had no idea if he was the kind of guy who would do something like that, but there were definitely plenty of guys at school who would. What if he was one of them?

Right away, my guard went up.

I'd gone through enough with boys because of my size. I wasn't about to risk that again, no matter how cute Nick St. James was.

Besides, there was a guy in Garland who truly liked me for me. He was the one I wanted to flirt with.

Nick said something about warming up later with a hot chocolate at Cocoa Corner. Before he could go on, I jumped in and said, "That sounds like fun. And I bet it'll warm you right up after being out in the snow so long."

He looked like he was about to ask me something, but I kept walking. "Well, I've got to get going. See ya."

"Yeah," he said, standing up straight again. "See you in school maybe."

I gave him one last wave and continued on my way.

Just a couple of weeks ago, I would've been absolutely ecstatic that Nick St. James was talking to me. Was that my Christmas wish at work? But how could it be when my heart already belonged to this year's Santa?

I shook off the weird feeling I had and kept walking toward town. I had a shift at the mall this afternoon, and I was looking forward to seeing Santa again. I missed his hand in mine and his laugh, the way his twinkling blue eyes saw more than my size—he saw me.

As I walked, my phone buzzed, and I stopped to pull it out of my pocket.

It was him.

Santa: See you later at the mall?

I texted back.

Belle: Yes, I'll be there.

The little bubbles popped up, and I waited for him to respond.

Santa: Can't wait to see you.

I grinned like an idiot, remembering to be careful and avoid the ice on the sidewalk as I walked. The last thing I needed was a broken arm or something because I was busy being distracted on cloud nine.

My phone buzzed again, and this time I stopped to look.

Santa: Want to go ice skating with me after work tonight?

I tapped out a quick message back.

Belle: Okay :)

I had no idea how our developing relationship would work with him unable to change out of his Santa costume, but I hoped he liked me enough to find a way.

Or maybe he'd finally show me who he really was?

## 17
## NICK

*I* had to tell her the truth.

I wasn't sure I could go one more day without doing so.

The more snow I shoveled, the more certain I felt.

If I could show Belle who I really was, then everything would be the way it was supposed to.

No more hiding. No more Santa costume standing in the way.

She could just be my girl, and she could know me as Nick, not the guy in the Santa suit. It was what I wanted more than anything in the world.

As I put away my shovel and headed back inside, I decided that telling her was the right thing to do. It wasn't right to keep progressing our relationship with such a big secret standing between us.

Running into her today like that and talking to her as Nick St. James almost felt like a sign. Now was our time. And nothing would stop me. I'd never felt like this about anyone.

I played the whole scenario out in my mind.

I could meet her tonight at the skating rink as myself, Nick St. James. I'd let her know ahead of time that I wouldn't be in the suit so she would be way less shocked about who I really was. And then we could spend time together as us.

Then everything would fall into place. I just knew it.

I exhaled, feeling tons of relief just at the thought of coming clean.

I'd really liked being Santa and getting to be anonymous in that suit, but not when it came to Belle. Not anymore. She'd proven that she didn't care about my status or just wanted to know me because I was a football star. She'd been kind and gotten to know me, even with a bushy beard and stick-on eyebrows covering my face.

Still, I wasn't sure we would've ended up where we were if it hadn't been for that suit.

If I hadn't been chosen as this year's Santa Claus and hadn't been in disguise, I had the feeling that everything that had happened between Belle and me... it might not have happened.

We wouldn't have been in the same place long enough to talk and get to know each other.

I wouldn't have had her incredible cookies either. I was pretty sure I'd fallen for her right then and there. The cute elf costume hadn't hurt either. Her hair. Her smile. Her sense of humor.

I might've never gotten to know Belle if it hadn't been for both of us working at the mall this year.

Whoever had picked me to be Santa, well, I definitely owed them one.

I couldn't wait to see her face when she saw the real me tonight at the ice-skating rink. And I couldn't wait to hold her hand and be with her as the real me. No more beard in the way of even more heart-pounding kisses...

The minutes seemed to tick by slower than ever, but finally, it was time to head to the mall. I took my usual route, which helped me avoid people, and I made my outfit change with plenty of time.

If Belle got there early, like she did sometimes, I

wanted to go ahead and see her. I was so excited to tell her the truth, I wondered if I could keep it in until tonight.

I made my way over near the food court and the Christmas tree.

The mall buzzed with families and kids ready to meet me at Santa's workshop. I stopped and took pictures more than once and waved at toddlers and babies.

Now that I'd had plenty of practice, I had the Santa walk and voice down pat.

When I got to the set, I looked around for Belle. Maybe she wasn't here yet after all. That was alright. It was better to stick to the plan and tell her later.

"Santa!" I heard behind me.

I spun around. It was one of the elves named Anna. She came over to me, a large white envelope in her hand. "This is for you. It got delivered earlier."

The pitch of her voice was high like an elf, which had to be a plus in this line of work.

I took it from her. "Thanks."

I looked at the envelope, seeing nothing on it except the words "For Santa" written in curling cursive.

But nothing showing who it was from.

Before I could ask Anna who gave her the letter, I realized she was gone.

I went and took a seat in my chair. The envelope felt thick, and I wanted to read what was inside. Maybe special instructions for today? It was getting really close to Christmas and busier than ever before.

A few people ran around, including Belle's mom, but I ignored all of them to open the envelope.

Inside was a thick sheet of paper. It was like the nice cardstock my mom used to send thank you notes to her clients.

*We would like to congratulate you on all your hard work so far. From the bottom of our hearts, thank you for bringing much Christmas magic to Garland's families and children this year.*

*Enclosed, please find a special gift from us to you.*

*Thank you again for keeping the secret and allowing us to keep this very special tradition of over a hundred years going. You are a part of the magic of our beloved town of Garland.*

*Signed: The Secret Santa Committee of Garland.*

That name matched the original package I had gotten, the one with my suit. Quickly, I looked up and glanced around. This had been from the committee? Were they watching me now? I couldn't help but wonder, even if the logical part of me knew that I'd never be able to tell if they were.

My gaze tracked an elderly man sitting at the fountain nearby. Was he on the committee? Had he dropped off this letter?

Then I noticed the lady at the cookie counter, wearing a bright green apron. She smiled at me. Could it be her?

I had no idea. I turned back to the letter.

Enclosed was a check for more money than I'd ever seen. And it looked like they'd made a special donation in my honor to Santa's Elves too. Mrs. Mulberry would be thrilled about that. It thrilled me too.

But even with more money than I could have hoped for, my heart sank because I knew now that I couldn't let Garland down.

I wouldn't be able to tell Belle who I really was after all. Ever.

There had to be another way to keep our relationship going, but no matter how much I racked my brain, I realized this tradition was bigger than just the two of us. Garland magic was something thousands of people enjoyed every year for more than a century. I knew the right thing to do, even if it tore me apart: I had to keep the secret.

18
BELLE

After a long day as an elf, I couldn't wait to meet Santa at the ice-skating rink.

I yawned and my stomach growled, but I changed into my cutest ice-skating outfit. Thick leggings, leg warmers, and a long knit sweater that I hoped would complement my eyes.

I wasn't the best skater in Garland, but hopefully, I would hold my own on the ice, maybe even skate around with him holding hands like I'd seen other couples do.

As I walked to the rink, Fall La La La La, I saw him standing underneath the red and green sign still dressed in his red and white velvet suit.

Getting closer to him, I nudged Santa playfully.

"Are you really going to skate in that suit?" I teased. And maybe part of me was disappointed too that I couldn't see the real him. There was this big secret looming between us, reminding me that something major was standing between me and my Christmas wish coming true.

Plus, this was the first time we'd really been out in public where a lot of people could see us, other than that time we walked to Cocoa Corner. It had at least been dark in the movie theater.

I had a feeling that ice skating together in public would be weird or raise a lot of questions or attract onlookers. That was the last thing I wanted. I just wanted us to hang out like normal, out of the spotlight.

Santa shrugged. "It's just for tonight. Besides, the skating rink is always empty on Tuesday nights."

That much was probably true. I was usually so busy baking this time of year, I didn't have a ton of time to come by.

He paid our way inside, and when we passed through to the rink, I could see that he was right. It wasn't as busy as it got on the weekends, but the people there still eyed us curiously.

Santa, who seemed to thrive in the spotlight, just waved and smiled and led me onto the ice. He was really good, effortlessly stepping onto the slick surface and spinning a few times. Maybe he was on the hockey team at school? I wondered which player he could be.

After a few minutes, I finally relaxed. We had a corner of the skating rink to ourselves, and it was getting emptier by the minute since the place would be closing soon.

But the music was great, upbeat Christmas music that made me want to sing my heart out like I was a Carol Karen or something. "I love this song," I called to him.

Santa whizzed past me, his long legs easily giving him speed. "Me too!"

The next time he came around, he grabbed my hand and we skated like that for the rest of the song. My heart fluttered thinking I was officially one of those girls who skated with the boy she liked. I followed his steps, adding in my own moves and twirls.

I'd taken lessons here as a kid, but it had been a while since I'd done anything too advanced.

Then Santa grabbed both of my hands, and we

spun around and around. I started laughing, holding on to him for dear life. Now the butterflies were partially from adrenaline too!

We slowed down, but then I made the mistake of letting his hands go for a second. I felt myself tumbling to the ice but not before he grabbed me.

He must've lost his balance too, though, because next thing I knew, I was lying on top of him. His chest was wide and firm and his eyes so close. He grinned. "Caught ya."

"My hero," I teased.

He grinned even wider. "Any time." How did I not recognize that smile?

I kept thinking I should get up, but another part of me didn't want to.

Santa was warm and sweet and kind, and I wanted us to stay like this forever, without the beard between us.

"Tell me who you really are?" I said. It came out before I could stop myself.

His grin slowly faded, and I began to wonder if I shouldn't have asked him that. But still, how could I keep kissing him and hanging out with him like this when I didn't even know who he was?

I deserved to know, didn't I?

"I won't tell anyone," I whispered. "Promise."

"I know you wouldn't," he finally replied. He reached up and brushed my hair back. "Believe me, I want to. So bad. I've thought about it over and over."

He didn't say anything for a bit, but before I could reply, he went on. "It's not about what I want though, Belle. It's about what I agreed to when I decided to put on this suit. It's about upholding one of Garland's most important traditions. People are counting on me."

Slowly, I got off of him and stood up. He stood up too.

I didn't get it. How could my Christmas wish be so close to coming true and yet so far away? My eyes stung with unshed tears. This felt so unfair.

All of a sudden, I wondered if the guy behind the beard was the right guy for me after all. Maybe he had nothing to do with my Christmas wish. All this time, I'd thought maybe the feelings growing between us meant my wish was coming true, but maybe that wasn't the case at all.

"Hey," he said, tilting my chin up toward him. "I'm sorry. I wish things were different."

"If they were, maybe we wouldn't be here," I said. It was the first thing that popped into my head, but it was true. A self-deprecating part of me wondered if he was only comfortable being seen with a big girl like me because of his disguise.

"You're right," he said. "I'm glad we met. I'm so glad for everything, Belle. I can't imagine what it would be like not to be your friend in real life."

Friend.

The word stung.

Was that what I was to him?

And he'd said "in real life." Did that mean this was all a game to him? Because it had been more than real to me.

My face felt hot and tears threatened to fill my eyes, but I swallowed and pushed them back.

No way was I going to cry in this moment.

Showing him just how much this all meant to me when it was all fun and games to him would be a thousand times worse than my Christmas wish never coming true.

"I should go," I said, making my voice sound normal. I began to skate toward the exit.

"Okay," he said, following me. "Let me walk you home."

I turned toward him and forced a smile. "It's okay. I'll see you later."

As I made my way home, I couldn't help but

think that maybe Christmas wishes like the one I'd made just didn't come true for girls like me.

I walked past Cocoa Corner, realizing that even a cup of hot cocoa wouldn't help me feel better.

## 19
## NICK

I hated the way Belle and I left things at the skating rink.

I stood at the railing, devastated, watching as she took off her skates and went home.

After walking to the bench and taking off my own skates, I texted her.

Santa: I'm sorry. Please let me know when you make it home.

No response.

Slowly, I pulled my boots on and left the rink. It was supposed to be a magical night, the night I told her who I really was, but now I didn't know if I'd be able to come back here without thinking of her and the sad look in her eyes.

The guy working closed up the skating rink behind me, giving me a silent wave as I walked out and the lights on the sign flickered off.

As I made my way home, my phone buzzed. My heart leapt as I fumbled through my pocket to check it.

Belle: Home.

That's all her message said.

She had to be mad at me, and understandably so. Maybe she thought I was embarrassed by her or just wanted to fool around with a winter fling. But it wasn't like that at all. I'd been so close to telling her the truth. So close, before realizing I couldn't do it.

It wasn't my secret to tell.

I got home, trudged to my room, and locked the door behind me.

"Nick, is that you?" Mom called from the kitchen.

I took off the thick red jacket. I had to swallow back the emotion in my throat before replying, "Yeah, Mom! Just need a quick shower!"

"Okay, dinner'll be ready in a few!" she called back.

I sighed, taking off my heavy leather boots. This sucked. I worried that Belle wouldn't want to speak to me again tomorrow or on Christmas Day.

It was like I was stuck between a rock and a hard place.

I knew she wouldn't tell anyone my secret, but I felt like I owed the committee to keep the promise I made when I put on the suit. Especially with how much they had paid me to do the job.

And besides, it would just take one slip, from me or her, for everyone to find out the truth. And that would basically ruin Christmas for a lot of kids in Garland. I wasn't sure I could live with that.

If I'd discovered one thing doing this job, it's that it was way more important than I originally thought.

This job wasn't just listening to kids tell me what they wanted for Christmas. It was about creating a space where kids could share what was really on their minds, make a wish, and experience the magic of the season.

Santa gave them hope and brought smiles to their faces.

Several parents told me so, including the mom

of one kid who was like me and had lost his dad young. Christmas was the one thing that had gotten him smiling and laughing again.

I couldn't risk ruining something like that. I wouldn't just ruin Christmas this year. I'd ruin it forever in Garland, and that's what made this town special.

Exhaling, I realized that's what it was. Protecting the Christmas magic for generations to come was what this was really about.

But how could I get Belle to see that it wasn't about keeping secrets from her or cutting our relationship short? I had no idea, now that we were both in so deep. She had to think I was a complete jerk.

I grabbed my phone again and texted her the only thing I could.

Santa: I'll think about it, okay?

## 20
## BELLE

Christmas Eve at the mall was tense and awkward with Santa. Even my mom noticed.

After hardly speaking a word to him all day, she came up to me, clipboard in hand and her walkie-talkie back in her belt. "You two okay?" she said, glancing at him. "You won't even look at him anymore."

I cast a glance his way, seeing him smile at a toddler sitting in his lap. The little boy grinned up at him, just as enamored with Santa and his charm as I was. But I couldn't tell my mom that I'd stupidly let myself fall for the one person who could never be fully honest with me about who he was.

"I'm fine. Why wouldn't I be?" I asked, sweeping up cookie crumbs from the floor.

"You and Santa have been inseparable since you started working here," she went on. "That's all."

I shrugged. "We're just friends. And this whole Santa thing is almost over anyway." I should just move on and let go of the childish wish I'd made.

"Okay," she said. "But he seems really nice."

I got what she was hinting at. It was probably obvious to everyone that we'd become close, but I wanted to make it clear that was no longer the case. "It was just an act for the sake of the town. Santa and his elf. He's a good actor."

"Hmm," Mom replied. She gave me a sad look that said she didn't believe me and walked away to help an elf that a baby just spat up on.

The truth was, it was easier to pretend it was all a game when it came to him than admit how crushed I was on the inside. I had really believed that my Christmas wish was going to come true and that my friends and I would find love this year. I'd thought I'd finally found a guy who liked me for me.

I hadn't had much time to talk to my friends, but I thought that if a relationship was really happening for me, then maybe it was for them too. But it seemed that wasn't the case at all.

I allowed myself a single lingering glance at Santa, then continued cleaning. How could you miss someone who was just feet away?

After our shift was over, he got out of his oversized velvet chair and walked my way. I hardly looked at him as I wiped down the benches nearby where families sat while they waited to see him.

"Hey," he said.

"Hi," I replied, focused on wiping off some stubborn and sticky juice from the bench.

"I understand if you're mad at me," he said.

I sprayed the cleaner again and kept scrubbing, moving on to the rest of the bench. I wasn't mad. I was hurt. Disappointed. Losing hope that I'd ever have a real relationship before I got out of high school. But since I couldn't tell him all that, I came up with a different reply. "Did you make a decision yet?" I asked, still not courageous enough to look at him.

He exhaled. "No, I haven't."

I stood up and finally faced him, paper towels and cleaning supplies in hand. "I understand."

"You do?" he asked.

I nodded. "I just want you to know I can't keep

doing this. Whatever this is." He cast his gaze down when I said that. "It's wrong for me to get my heart so involved with you when it can only go so far. It's not fair." My voice broke a little when I said that last part, and I focused on swallowing and steadying my gaze on him. "I hope you understand."

Then I left. I didn't want to stick around and draw this out any longer than necessary. Knowing everything that happened between us was over hurt enough.

I finished the last of my tasks for the day, changed out of my elf costume, and headed home as quickly as I could, ready for all this hurt to be behind me. For the first time in my life, I was ready for Christmas to be over.

I texted Mom, letting her know I'd see her at home.

She would be home soon, with it being Christmas Eve. Most of Garland would shut down this evening, except for a select few places. Almost everyone would be with family, enjoying each other's company and eating lots of food.

Maybe I'd go home and bake another batch of cookies before we started our Christmas Eve tradition. I could go around and visit a few people tomorrow and hand them out to spread some Christmas cheer, despite not feeling any at the moment. Anything to get my mind off of Santa and the ache he left in my heart.

I walked in the door, glad my dad and brother weren't home to see me holding back tears as I took off my hat and gloves. Then I went to the couch and curled up with Yeti, running my fingers through his puffy white fur. He rested his head on my chest like he could tell how much I was hurting.

This had to be the most terrible Christmas to date. Which sucked because it could've been one of the best. But I reminded myself that even with everything that had happened, there was still so much to be grateful for. My parents, my brother, my dog, and my friends. Garland itself. The lights. Hot chocolate and cookies that filled our bellies.

Even with all those blessings, my heart ached for the one thing I didn't have, the one thing that felt so close yet so out of reach: the boy with the bright blue eyes in the Santa suit.

I was losing him for good.

## 21
## NICK

*I* tried not to let Belle's words bring me down, but every time I thought about her voice breaking and the tears in her eyes, I couldn't help but feel bad.

Her words had stung, but what had been worse was seeing how obviously hurt she was because of me. When I'd taken on this job, I just hadn't counted on something like this happening.

How had things become so complicated between us?

I just wanted to go back to the day at the movies when we'd kissed under the falling snow, her nose cold but her lips warm.

I wondered if we'd ever be able to go back to

that. Things weren't looking good. That I knew for sure.

Would I ever get to tell her the truth? Part of me was certain it was too late.

Trying to put it out of my mind, I changed out of my Santa suit and back into civilian attire.

I had some last-minute holiday shopping to do. I'd hoped that maybe Belle would join me because I had one more special gift to buy that I knew she'd be able to help me with, but now I was on my own.

Back at the mall, I walked around the mall for a while, feeling kind of hopeless and distracted. Nothing I saw seemed like quite the right gift for my mom.

Sighing, I put down the large vanilla-scented candle. She deserved something special.

After looking at cookware and vacuums at the department store, I was about ready to give up and get her a store gift card. I left the mall, tempted to sit and be a grump with a cup of eggnog at Scrooge's. So much for holiday spirit.

Then I spotted Vixen's. Mom got her nails done there a few times a year as a special treat. It was her favorite splurge.

That was it.

With a little extra boost of energy, I walked in, bells chiming behind me.

"Hey, Nick, how can we help you today?" Mrs. Katz smiled at me from behind the counter. She wore a bright green apron and there were several ladies behind her getting manicures or a massage.

"Afternoon, Mrs. Katz. I'm looking to get something nice for my mom," I said, coming up the counter.

She smiled, and it reached her eyes. "Well, isn't that sweet of you?" she said. "How is your mother?"

"Good," I replied politely. "Just staying busy as usual."

She gave me another nice smile. "I tell Jessica every time I see her that she works too much. Just about the hardest working person I know."

"Yes, ma'am, she is," I said. "Which is why I thought she might like a spa day or something as a Christmas gift."

She lit up. "I have just the thing." She pulled out a nice brochure. It had a gift card inside. "This is our deluxe spa day package."

Mrs. Katz pulled out some lotions and things too. "And it comes with this nice basket of luxury personal care items."

She went on for a minute about what was included for the price. I understood less than half of what she was saying, but I was sure Mom would blow a gasket when she saw everything.

"And I'll tell you what," she said. "I'll throw in a bonus mani-pedi day too. Jessica deserves it. She always did come by with a casserole or two when my little Rosie was born."

I grinned. That was Mom, alright. Always thinking of everyone else but herself. "I'll take it. Thank you very much."

"Great. I'll wrap this up for you," she said.

I walked out of there feeling way better than when I'd left the mall. At least Mom would have a nice Christmas this year.

The next morning, I woke up bright and early, only to find Mom already whipping up a big breakfast.

I set her gift down under the tree. My gift was already there, wrapped and ready to be opened.

Mom came out with a large mug of coffee and a big hug for me. "Merry Christmas, honey."

"Merry Christmas, Mom," I said, hugging her back.

We sat and opened our gifts. She cried when she opened the present I got her.

"What did I do to deserve a son like you?" she said, wiping at her eyes with the gift in her lap.

She'd gotten me a new pair of football cleats, which was good because my old ones were starting to fall apart. I opened the other gift. It was some sort of photo album, with tons of pictures inside. There were pictures of the three of us, when Dad had still been around. Then tons of me and her. And several more still of just me.

"You took a lot of pictures," I said.

"I wanted to capture every moment," she replied.

I ran my finger over one of the photos of me on the ice in a too-big coat. "I forgot I used to skate so much."

"That's how you started volunteering at Santa's Elves, remember? The skating park is just down the block."

"Oh yeah," I said, remembering. "Wow. Thanks, Mom. This is great."

"I know you probably feel misunderstood at times, but I also see what a big heart you have." She touched my cheek. "I'll always be here for you, Nick."

I leaned in and hugged her. "Thanks, Mom. I'll always be here too."

She started crying again, and we both ended up laughing when I poked fun at her for it.

I couldn't help but think about Belle as we sat and ate breakfast.

I would've done about anything to see her again, wish her a merry Christmas, and have just a little bit of what we'd had before.

## 22
## BELLE

*I* woke up on Christmas Day and stared out my window. There was fresh snow on the ground, and the sun shone bright. I smiled before everything that had happened recently jumped to the forefront of my mind.

I went through the motions that morning, doing my best to enjoy Christmas with my family.

Dylan got a new PlayStation, which he plugged in right away. I got some baking supplies, including a special cookbook I'd been eyeing for a long time and some unique new cookie cutters.

Opening presents always brought a smile to my face. My parents always gave us the best gifts, but after we were done, I couldn't help but think that there was one thing I likely wasn't going to get this Christmas after all.

And that was seeing my Christmas wish come true. There were just a few more hours left, and short of a Christmas miracle... Well, it was time to let it go.

We had our traditional Christmas Day lunch of giant turkey sandwiches from yesterday's leftover roast turkey, and then I got ready for my last shift at the mall.

A celebration and party, really.

The mall would be open but just so everyone could come by and say goodbye to Santa and his elves before they set off for the North Pole again.

I pulled on my elf hat, bundled up, and set off for Cider Center. It was probably going to be awkward seeing Santa, but the faster I could get this over with, the better. Leave it all behind, from the sweet, fun memories to the heartbreak.

Maybe I'd see Bethany or Holly there. For sure we'd all be together for New Year's Eve, and that was something to look forward to.

As soon as I got to the mall, I wished I was back home, baking and blissfully ignoring everything that had happened the past few days.

I stood with all the other elves near the chair

where Santa Claus sat as the mayor himself dropped in to congratulate us on a job well done.

"Three thousand," Mom said, microphone in hand. "That's how many children and families you made a difference for this year. I hope you're all proud of the incredibly important work you did this holiday season."

The mayor began clapping wholeheartedly, and we all joined in. My heart lit up. It was worth all the clean-up, crazy kids, and long hours. Even the heartbreak.

Mom handed the mayor the mic. He addressed us, looking around. "I really do hope you're proud of the work you've done for the town of Garland. I know I'm proud." Everyone clapped at his remark. "Our citizens and families are proud, and you're the reason for this year's magical Christmas season." He glanced at Santa Claus, who sat in his chair several feet away from me, clapping and joining in as well. "And I hear that this year's Santa is the best we've ever had, which is really saying something. Please join me in thanking him." He set the mic aside and began clapping. We all joined in, and I finally chanced a glance at Santa. He stood up and gave a humble bow.

When the clapping finally died down, Mom

told us to eat and drink up. This party was for us. The music came on and the elves and other workers dispersed, talking excitedly and getting in line for food.

I talked to a couple of the girls my age who I'd gotten to know more during my shifts here, but mostly, I wanted to head back home.

Mom wanted to walk home together, though, so I stuck around a little while longer.

It wasn't long before everyone was ready to go home. I was itching to get back into my thick Christmas pj's and crawl into bed. Maybe text my friends for a little while.

I saw Santa hang around and talk to some of the elves and even the mayor, and I made sure to stay away. Talking to him wouldn't fix anything. That I knew.

But when I walked toward the back room to wait in Mom's office, I was surprised to hear a "Belle, wait!" behind me.

I turned back and saw Santa approaching me. He entered the hallway that led to Mom's office. I froze, wondering what he wanted.

"Hey," he said, finally coming to a stop in front of me.

"Hey," I said quietly.

"Listen, I know I'm probably the last person you want to talk to right now, but I just wanted to…" He slowed down, his brows knitting together. "I just wanted us to say goodbye before we go back to our regular lives."

I realized what he already knew. This was it. The last time I would ever see him.

Maybe he would see me. He'd recognize me. But I would not recognize him. We would just be two normal people with some history.

"I'm sorry for the way things ended, Belle," he went on. "But I'm not sorry for everything that happened between us."

Before I could say anything, he reached down and kissed me on the cheek. For a second, I thought he might start really kissing me, like that time outside with snow falling all around us.

But he didn't.

"Bye," I managed.

And then he was gone.

## 23
## NICK

When I got back home, there was a large package at the door.

I picked it up. It was empty but with writing on the front. It looked like the postage was paid for and the delivery address filled out.

That's when I figured out what it was.

I went inside and closed the front door behind me with a sigh.

"Nick, is that you?" Mom called from her room.

"Yeah, Mom," I replied. I went into my room and shut the door. I pulled out the Santa costume from my large duffel bag. So this was it. Time for it to go back.

I held it up and admired it one more time. The

soft dark red velvet. The thick white (really realistic) beard. The hat and the boots.

This was the best thing that had ever happened to me. Even so, my chest ached with all that had happened with Belle. I missed her already, and I had no idea how to get her back.

Carefully, I folded up the suit and put it in the box. Then the boots and everything else. *They had to have some sort of special dry-cleaning service for this thing*, I thought. Otherwise, it would've stunk to high heaven by now, like my football uniform.

I closed up the box, and before I could think too much about it, I headed to the post office. It wasn't far, and I needed some time to think. I shot Mom a quick text so she wouldn't worry. The sooner this suit got back to where it belonged, the better.

It had been an honor to wear it. I never would've imagined that I'd get that honor, and it had been the experience of a lifetime. But now it was time to give it back. Someone else would do it next year and get to experience the magic. Create some magic of their own too.

Since it was Christmas Day, just about everything was closed, including the Garland post office. I set the box right at the drop box since it was already labeled and had postage. I knew Mr. Long would find it in the morning.

I looked at the unassuming brown package, feeling the strange desire to pick it up and take it back home with me.

Deep down, I wasn't ready to let go of the one thing that still tied me to Belle. Because I knew leaving this Santa suit behind would be proof that it all was over. Our hot cocoa dates. Kissing outside the movie theater. Holding hands. Seeing her smile and being truly known by her. It was all over.

But I couldn't hold on to the suit either. It was what brought us together and what kept us apart all at the same time. And even though I had to keep the secret, the red velvet costume wasn't mine. Not anymore.

I took a shaky breath, blinking quickly, and turned around to walk back home.

The whole way there, I thought about Belle and what would happen next.

I wanted her in my life, but I also knew it wouldn't be right for me to get to know her again as Nick St. James like nothing had happened between us. There would always be a secret if I did that. But I also couldn't tell her the truth. That's what had gotten us here in the first place.

No matter how much I thought about our situation or how many angles I tried to see it from, I just didn't see a way we could have what we had before.

From now on, I would see her around town and pass her in the hallways at school and it would be completely different. I couldn't tell who it would be worse for—me, knowing who she was, deep down, and knowing I couldn't have her. Or her, who'd never know just how close Santa really was.

If a reality existed where I got to hold her in my arms again or brush her hair back, maybe it would have to be years in the future. Maybe only then. If she hadn't already found someone else.

Just thinking about that possibility really made my heart feel as cold as the snow crunching under my boots.

When I got back home, I was so upset I couldn't go inside because I knew my mom would ask questions. Questions I couldn't answer–and I couldn't stand keeping any more secrets. So I got out the snow shovel. It had snowed last night, and with everything going on, I hadn't gotten to it yet.

And right now, what I needed was some mind-numbing work.

I held the wooden handle in my gloved hands and focused on the scrape of metal over cement. It was time to go back to my normal life, with snow shoveling, volunteering on Saturdays at Santa's Elves, hanging out with my friends, and pretty soon, going back to being the star quarterback of the high school football team. My old life would have to be enough.

Everything that had happened with Belle had been special, but it looked like it wasn't something I'd get to keep in my life after all.

## 24
## BELLE

Mom handed me a letter as I came out of my room to eat breakfast. "Mail for you, sweetie."

I took the envelope from her, confused. "For me?" No one ever sent me mail; everyone I knew preferred to text or send emails. But when I looked at the white paper and the stamp decorated with a Christmas tree, I found my name was right there at the top.

I sat down at the kitchen table to open it while Yeti followed me and sat at my feet. Who would be writing me a letter?

My first thought went to Santa, my heart aching with hope. But I pushed him out of my mind. We had agreed it was over. And as I looked at the letter inside the envelope, I saw that the letter wasn't from Santa at all.

It was from Scrooge at the diner, wanting to order a batch of cookies. A few crisp twenty-dollar bills stared up at me.

I looked between the letter and the money, trying to make sense of it. I'd never told him that I had cookies for sale…

I kept reading, taking in his neat, slanted handwriting. He wanted an order of several dozen decorated sugar cookies to start. He wanted to add them to his display case and see if his customers liked them. He asked if I could have the cookies ready within the week, and said to call him if I needed more time.

"Who is it from?" Mom asked, setting a bowl of oatmeal in front of me and peeking over my shoulder. I handed her the letter while sniffing the maple cinnamon oatmeal. It made my mouth water.

"You're selling batches of cookies now?" she asked, setting the letter on the table beside my bowl. "Good for you."

"I didn't know I was," I muttered, reading the letter again.

She went back to making breakfast for Dad and

my brother, who were the late risers in our family, while my thoughts went back to Santa again. He had told me that he and his mom went to Scrooge's every year on Christmas Day. Was this his doing?

Maybe he really did care for me like I cared for him. My heart dangerously hoped it wasn't just a fling.

I bit my lip as tears welled up in my eyes.

The truth was that I missed him so much. That final goodbye with him had crushed me, especially because he'd taken the news so well, hardly any emotion showing in his deep blue eyes.

But this cookie order had to be him. He's the only one who knew about my dreams of opening a bakery one day, besides Mom.

I wiped away a single tear that rolled down my cheek.

What should I do?

Mom seemed to answer for me as she sat across from me at the table with her own bowl of oatmeal. "So, sounds like you're going to spend the morning baking?"

I stood up and nodded. "Yeah, I guess."

She patted me on the arm as I walked past her

with my half-empty bowl. "Good for you, hon," she said.

After rinsing out my bowl, I got everything ready, determined to make the best batch of cookies for my first order. I gathered all my ingredients and began measuring everything out. Even though Christmas had passed, I played Christmas music softly in the background. The rule in this household—and most of Garland—was that we pretty much played Christmas music from November 1 to February 1. That was about the time people took down their trees too. Most people, anyway.

But Christmas music didn't seem as happy today as it usually did. As I began making the dough, I noticed my mind kept drifting back to Santa. More than ever, I wished I just knew his real name. My heart hurt as I used the special machine he gave me to form the cookie shapes. I couldn't even tell him thank you for getting me my first order–if it was really him behind this.

Would I think about him every Christmas for the rest of my life? Every time I got a cookie order?

I sighed and took a step back to look at my work. Probably.

My dad and brother woke up a little later,

coming in and out of the kitchen while I baked the cookies and prepped the frosting. Within a few hours, the cookies were ready. And I had to admit... They looked perfect.

I packaged them up in cookie tins we had on hand, making a mental note to order some special boxes and labels I could use going forward. Especially if Scrooge was going to be a regular customer. Now I had money to invest back into the business.

My business.

Now that I had my first paying customer (hopefully, repeat customer), I officially had a business.

I smiled but also felt another tear run down my cheek.

I took a picture of the order for memory's sake and headed down to Scrooge's to drop them off, thinking about what I would name my bakery one day. "Belle's Bakery"? "Sleigh Belles" to go with Garland's Christmas theme? Or maybe "Santa's Cookies" in memory of the boy who was my first crush and the first to support my business as more than a "one day" dream.

It took about fifteen minutes to walk to Scrooge's Diner, the one business on Main Street devoid of any type of Christmas decorations. In fact, the only thing even close to holiday spirit was the bells over the door that jingled as I walked inside.

A few people ate at tables. My heart sank thinking of Santa here with his mom on Christmas Day. He'd been in this place, sat in one of these chairs, and maybe one day he would eat one of my cookies from the display, but that was as close as we'd ever get again.

I shoved aside my sad thoughts, focusing instead on this moment. On the fact that I was delivering my very first order.

I walked up to the counter, a smile on my face as I approached Scrooge drying coffee mugs and stacking them on trays. He was a handsome older man, about my parents' age, with dark brown hair and short stubble on his chin.

"I have your cookies ready," I told him, setting the tins in front of him.

He thanked me gruffly when I did. "That was fast."

"Thank you for the order," I replied.

He pulled open the lid on one of the tins and said, "These look great." He began taking them out to put in the empty glass display.

I went around the corner and helped him, carefully arranging them so it was easy to see the pretty designs I'd put on them. Since I knew he didn't like Christmas, I'd made them all scalloped circle shapes with pretty white designs. The icing sugar caught the light, making them shimmer.

A tall guy, maybe a little younger than my dad, came up to the counter to pay for his meal. "Are those fresh cookies for sale?"

"Yes!" I said.

"I'll take three and a coffee," he replied, sliding into a seat at the counter.

Scrooge gave him a plate with three cookies and poured a fresh cup. "Enjoy."

I couldn't leave, not now with the first customer about to try them.

The man picked one up and took a bite. "Wow, these are as good as my grandmother used to make them."

Scrooge turned to me. "How about another batch next week?"

I grinned. "You got it, Scrooge."

He smirked at the nickname, then left from behind the counter to tend to the rest of his customers, and I turned back to the display case, making sure the cookies looked perfect and adding a nice handwritten sign too from a scrap of paper and marker that I found nearby.

"There," I said, admiring my work.

Now that I had my first customer, maybe I could find another one.

But who did I have to thank for this one? Who was Santa?

I turned back to Scrooge, who was busy getting drinks for people at the tables. I knew it was as easy as asking him, but I couldn't bring myself to do it.

Santa hadn't wanted to tell me. Even told me he *couldn't*. And this wasn't the way I wanted to find out. If we were to have a relationship, I would want him to tell me himself.

But as I looked around the shop, saw the diner finishing his first cookie, I knew I would think of Santa every Christmas and how he helped me start my bakery.

## 25
## NICK

Mom and I found ourselves at Scrooge's again the day after Christmas.

We had come here for Christmas dinner and hung out with Scrooge and a couple other Christmas regulars. But Scrooge had the best burgers, fries, and milkshakes in town, so I wasn't upset when Mom had suggested coming here again for supper.

I think she thought that Scrooge was lonely, but I was starting to think that maybe she was kind of lonely too and enjoyed his company.

In one more year, I'd be off to college, and while I didn't want to go far, I knew it wouldn't be the same as me living at home. She'd be on her own.

We sat down at the counter, and I picked up the menu even though I knew I would get the same thing I always did—a burger with onion rings.

Right away, Scrooge came over to wipe down the counter next to us and refill the sugar packets. But I think he just wanted to talk to Mom. Or listen to her talk, really.

I noticed how her face lit up as she conversed with him, and for the first time, I noticed Scrooge too. It was like I could sense his heart growing a size or two. The man wasn't bad-looking at all, as far as potential guys to date my mom went. And I could tell my mom was trying not to stare.

He was a little rough around the edges, with stubble that covered most of his jaw, and he didn't like to socialize much, even though he ran the diner. But he had a quiet kindness if he allowed you to get close enough to see it.

Scrooge turned to me. "What'll you have to drink, Nick?"

"Root beer, please," I replied.

"And for me too," Mom said with a smile on her face.

Scrooge nodded in response and turned to get us drinks from the fountain machine. Mom asked him a question about his shirt, wondering if he had gotten it for Christmas. To me it looked the same as what he usually wore.

Figuring Mom might appreciate a few minutes on her own, I excused myself to the bathroom. As I walked past the cash register, I noticed the large display case off to the side. It was full of very familiar-looking cookies.

My lips lifted even though an ache settled in my chest. The sight of them reminded me so much of Belle. I knew it was weird of me to stand there staring at the cookies, so I continued to the restroom.

When I took my seat again a few minutes later, Scrooge was polishing an already sparkling-clean glass and listening to Mom talk about something or other. "I see you got the cookies in already," I told him at a break in their conversation.

He nodded and kept cleaning the glass in his hand. "Yeah, thanks for the tip. People love 'em."

"Have you had one?" I asked him, taking a sip of my root beer.

"Yep," Scrooge said. "They don't make 'em like that anymore, I'll tell you that. Reminds me of…" He paused for a moment, then seemed to remember he was talking out loud. "Anyway, I've already put in another order." He finally finished polishing the glass, setting it carefully on the shelf behind him. "That girl should open a bakery or something."

A few people came in the door, and Scrooge set off to take care of them.

Mom turned to me, picking up her root beer. "Is it me or is Scrooge a little nicer these days?"

"With you," I teased. "I don't think I've ever heard him say more than one full sentence, until now." I grinned. "I think he has a crush on you, Mom."

She nudged me playfully, but I saw the color rising in her cheeks like she was the teenager and not me.

I put my drink down and glanced at the display case. While I wanted to taste one of Belle's cookies again, I also wished she was the one giving it to me, because that would mean she wasn't mad at me anymore.

That things weren't over between us.

Mom nudged me again. This time concern etched her face. "What is it?"

I opened my mouth but didn't quite know what to say. "It's nothing, Mom," I said finally.

"I don't think it's nothing," she said. "I've never seen you like this, honey. What is it?"

I sighed. "Belle, the girl who bakes the cookies," I began but didn't know how to go on without telling my mom about the Santa suit and the reason why Belle and I broke up.

"I thought there might be a reason you were out of the house so much this last week," Mom said. "Is there something going on between you two?"

"There was." I shook my head. "Not anymore."

"Oh," Mom said, taking a sip of her root beer. "What happened?"

I slowly spun my own cup on the counter, watching condensation rings reflect the fluorescent lights. "I can't really say, Mom. I wish I could, but…"

Mom's brow furrowed. "Why not?"

"I just… I made a promise I can't break, and because of that, I can't really pursue things with Belle."

Mom took another sip of her root beer. She looked at me like she was worried I'd gotten myself into trouble of some kind.

"I promise it's nothing bad," I said. "In fact, it's the opposite. It's something really good. A really good reason that's keeping me from having a relationship with her ever again."

Mom seemed to relax a little after that even though she still looked doubtful, like she wanted to ask me a million more questions, but thankfully she didn't because Scrooge came by with our food, setting our plates in front of us, along with our favorite dipping sauces.

After Mom thanked him and he walked away, she said to me, "Well, I don't know what all is going on, Nick, but I do know that you're a good person and I trust you."

Her words had a lump forming in my throat. It was hard to feel like a good person with Belle's hurt expression on replay in my mind. "Thanks, Mom," I managed.

"But I can also tell this is really upsetting you," she continued. "I won't ask too many questions, but I will tell you this. We lost your dad over ten years ago now." Her voice broke a little as she said it and tears welled up in her eyes, but she went on. "Even with how hard it was to lose him, not one day goes by that I'm not thankful for all the time we had together. You should never let your feelings for someone go unspoken. Time is a precious thing."

My chest felt tight as she talked about Dad. His absence was extra hard this time of year because he loved the Christmas season. I squeezed her hand. "I know, Mom, but I–"

"I know what you're about to say," she said. "That you don't have a choice. That may be so, but I also know that there's always a way, especially when it comes to the special people in our lives." She squeezed my hand back. "There's always a way, Nick. You just have to find one."

## 26
## BELLE

Mom sat down next to me on the couch, a fresh cup of hot coffee in hand. "You're pretty quiet lately," she said. "And you haven't hung out with your friends like you usually do."

I exhaled and shrugged my shoulders, hardly looking up from some cookie decoration ideas I was doodling in my journal. If I did, she might see how upset I really was. "They've all been busy. We all have, I guess," I added. "I'll probably see them for New Year's."

"Got big plans?" Mom asked, settling into the couch, Yeti sitting between us.

I bit my lip before answering, "Not really." I'd been thinking of going to Haley's big New Year's

Eve party—everyone in school went each year. But I didn't know if I could handle going and seeing everyone kiss their crush at midnight.

We were quiet for a minute before she finally said, "You seem different, honey. Like you're upset about something."

There was a beat of silence, just the TV playing quietly in the background, but neither of us were paying attention to it.

"You know you can tell me if something's bothering you," she went on.

I looked at her, thinking it might feel good to talk to someone about this. "There was a boy."

"Was?" she asked, gaze completely focused on me. "There isn't anymore?"

I shook my head. "It got complicated really fast."

She looked at me kind of funny, and I knew she had probably already pieced most of it together. I mean, she had seen us talk and hang out a lot at Cider Center. "This wouldn't be a certain someone who happened to wear a red suit, would it?"

I didn't have to respond for her to know the answer. I set my journal down, giving up on the designs.

She nodded knowingly and patted my knee. "I see."

"He made a promise he can't break," I told her.

"About who he really is," Mom finished for me.

Tears welled up in my eyes, and I swallowed to keep them at bay. "Yeah." I missed him, and it had only been two days. What if I never saw him again? Or worse, saw him without knowing who he really was? Would I spend the rest of my life wondering if each blue-eyed person was him?

Now she bit her lip, and I could tell she was thinking.

"There's not much we can do," I said. I had turned it around in my head over and over again, always coming to the same conclusion. Garland may be a magical place to live, but right now, the Secret Santa tradition didn't feel so great.

Mom exhaled, her eyes focusing on the freshly falling snow outside the living room window. "So he can't tell you who he is, even now." She kept thinking. "What if one of you wrote a letter to the Secret Santa Committee of Garland, asking for special permission?"

I sat up, brows furrowed. "The what?"

"The Secret Santa Committee of Garland.

They're the ones who elect the person who will be Santa each year."

I blinked. I'd never really thought about how Santa was selected. "Who's on the committee?"

"It's a secret, silly. I'm not sure anyone knows who they are, at least not the whole committee. But I've had my suspicions over the years, and I think I might know a way to reach them."

Hope filled my chest. "Really? But what would I tell them?"

"Ask them to help you make a little extra Christmas magic before the year is over," Mom said, a soft smile on her lips. "It's worth at least pleading your case, don't you think? You never know."

I thought about her idea. It made a lot of sense, but I was also afraid to hope, only to be disappointed.

Mom grabbed my hand. "Think about it, Belle. Where does the Christmas magic in Garland come from?"

I looked at her. "The Christmas star?" I tried, thinking of the pretty star atop the giant tree–the one we all made our wishes on. Legend said it had been gifted to Garland by Santa himself.

She gave my hand a squeeze. "The people." Her

eyes did that thing where they got big and bright. Convincing. This was why she was the best manager Cider Center had ever had. She could get people on board with her ideas when she really believed in them. "The people of Garland create the magic from how much they care about and love each other. I've seen it time and time again. Other places have lost that over the years, but not Garland."

Something inside me told me she was right. "Okay," I said slowly. "So what do I do?"

"Write a letter to the committee," she said, standing up. "And I'll make sure they get it."

After she left, I sat there for a minute, trying to process everything she'd just told me. Was there really a chance for some extra Christmas magic?

A chance for my wish to really come true?

I felt like I had no other choice but to hope just a little bit longer.

I tore away the page in my journal with my doodles so that I had a fresh page. Then I picked up my pen and began writing.

## 27
## NICK

New Year's Eve was right around the corner, and all everyone could talk about was the big party at Haley's house.

But all I could think about was Belle, how much I missed her, and what Mom had said about there always being a way.

The day after our conversation, I was lying in bed, bored and missing the Christmas season at the mall, when it hit me.

The committee had been able to communicate with me through the post office. What if I could communicate back?

I had no idea what they would say to the idea of me letting Belle in on my big secret, but what I knew for sure was that I had to try.

If I didn't, it was guaranteed that I'd never get her back.

But if I wrote to them... then maybe I had a chance of fixing this. Of having a real relationship with her, not as Santa, but as Nick St. James.

I dug through my school bag waiting in my closet, found a pen and sheet of paper, and made my way to the kitchen table. My room was hardly big enough for my bed and dresser, let alone a desk, so I always did my homework in the kitchen anyway, ever since I was little.

I sat there, pen in hand, not knowing where to start. I glanced over at my goldfish, watching him swim about his tank for a moment while I thought over my words.

*Dear Secret Santa Committee of Garland,*

*My name is Nick St. James. Also known as this year's Secret Santa. But you already knew that.*

*I'm writing to you today for two reasons.*

*One, to say thank you. I never would've guessed that I would be selected and have the honor of doing this job. It changed my perspective, and I'm truly grateful for the experience, knowing I got to participate in one of Garland's most sacred traditions. Seeing how happy it made the children in town was worth more than any present I could get under the tree.*

*Two, I want to ask for a favor. I want to break the rules and tell one very special person that it was me behind the beard and the suit. Please allow me to explain why...*

I EXHALED AND KEPT WRITING.

Before long, I was on my way to the post office, my letter carefully folded and sealed in an envelope. I couldn't help but think that my letter probably sounded stupid. Maybe they wouldn't even get it, but I had to try and hope my mom was right—that there was a way for Belle and me to be together.

My hands were cold and so were my ears. I'd been so focused on getting this letter to the post office that I'd forgotten to grab my hat and gloves.

I stood outside the brick building, in front of the blue metal letter drop box, hoping Mr. Long would know how to get my letter to the right place. I looked at the front of the envelope one more time. It was addressed to the Secret Santa Committee of Garland. There was no return address. They would know it was me. They would know how to get in touch. But hopefully, this letter actually got to them in the first place. Otherwise, I had no idea how else I could reach them.

Finally, I dropped my letter in, shoved my hands in my pockets to warm them up, and made my way back home.

The whole time I kept thinking: *Where was Belle now? Would I get to tell her the truth?*

## 28
## BELLE

I sat at my favorite booth inside Cocoa Corner, the same one Santa and I had shared, a cup of hot cocoa in front of me. Even though it was my favorite drink in the world, I could hardly stomach it. Being here brought up too many happy-turned-painful memories, which I hadn't realized until sitting down.

I sighed and stared out the window. A cute couple walked past, hand in hand. So much for my wish. Maybe some people got to have that sort of thing and others didn't.

It had been a couple days since I'd handed Mom the letter, and so far, nothing. Pretty sure Mom was already tired of me asking her if she'd heard back yet, only to answer and say she hadn't.

But as I sat here, in this place where he once made me feel so special, a new fear washed over me... What if he'd already moved on?

I hadn't seen or heard from him since Christmas, as Santa or his real self. But while I'd been spending all this time mourning what could never be, maybe he hadn't thought of me at all. That ate me up almost as much as knowing he could pass by me on the sidewalk without me ever knowing.

The more I thought about it, the more I wondered if I had even done the right thing by sending the letter. Even if the committee said it was okay, would he want me to know? And if they said okay and he didn't come forward... I didn't want to think about how that would feel. It was too late to go back now.

I got up and went to the restroom, thinking it was probably time for me to go home. Maybe start baking the next batch of cookies for Scrooge. If word got around, who knew? Maybe I could have a few more customers like him.

Not too many since I still had school, but the idea of socking away money for a future bakery really lit me up. That's what I had to hold on to, as much as it hurt to remember everything that had happened. Even if it had led to this.

When I got back, I was surprised to find a letter next to my still-hot cup of cocoa. I glanced over at the counter, seeing one of the owners of Cocoa Corner, Jack Lumi, wiping down the espresso machine.

I went over to him, holding up the crisp, creamy white envelope with a bump in the middle. It felt expensive. "Hey, is this from you?" I asked.

He shook his head. "No. I was in the back."

"Hmm," I said, looking around the shop. Everyone there seemed to be involved in their own conversations or computers.

I glanced down at the envelope again, turning it over to see if there was a return address or something as I walked back to my booth. But as I sat down, all I saw was "Belle" on the front in curling black calligraphy.

I wondered what was inside just as much as I wondered who left it.

I peeled back the envelope flap, finding a silver sleigh bell in there. I turned it over in my hand, hearing the soft, metallic tinkle of the bell. Setting it in front of me, I pulled out the letter inside.

It was just a small card, telling me to be at Cider Center in front of the Christmas tree at 3 p.m. today.

My brow furrowed. It didn't say why or who this was from. I checked the back of the card. Nothing.

I looked around the shop again, but I didn't see anyone watching me.

This was odd.

Then it dawned on me.

The letter I'd sent to the committee. Had they gotten it? Was this their response?

Were they going to meet me and let me know their decision?

I checked the time. It was 2:47 p.m.

I could be there in just a few minutes if I left now.

My heart rate sped as I got up from my booth, slipping my coat back on. The door to Cocoa Corner closed behind me with a soft ding. It almost matched the ding of the sleigh bell in my hand.

My heart raced even faster as I walked to the Cider Center, wondering what would happen, who would be waiting for me there.

Some old gentlemen who were part of the committee maybe? Another note? What would they say? I braced myself for disappointment, someone waiting to let me down easy, despite the hope fluttering in my chest.

I could hardly think straight, but in just a few minutes, I was there.

Cider Center and Garland Mall weren't super busy, with just a few people milling around. Some kids ran and played near the tree as they made their way to the mall with their parents.

I glanced around, wondering who or what to look for. So far, no one seemed to be waiting for me.

I checked the time again. 2:58 p.m.

There was a large bench nearby, but I knew I wouldn't be able to sit and wait.

Instead, the star at the top of the tree caught my eye. I locked my gaze on it, going back to the moment when I'd made that wish a couple weeks ago.

I had probably asked for far too much. Now, here I stood again, heartbroken. Maybe it would be mended by the time I stood here again next year. Or maybe I should learn my lesson and not make a wish at all.

"Belle?" I heard.

I spun around at the sound of my name behind me.

The sleigh bell was still in my hand. It made a sound as I faced the person who had called my name.

My eyes went from his face to the sleigh bell in his hand in less than a second.

He held it up. It made a gentle ringing sound.

I did the same, not believing who stood in front of me.

Nick St. James smiled and took a step toward me. "I can't believe this."

"Nick?" I said, in shock. Nick St. James had been the boy behind the beard? The one wearing the Santa suit this whole time?

"It's me," he replied.

It didn't make sense. The most popular guy in school? He was the one I'd been talking to this whole time? The one who'd kissed me? His voice was familiar, but his eyes?

His eyes said it all. They were the same sparkling blue eyes I'd gotten to know so well.

"I'm guessing the committee got my letter after all," he said, pulling an envelope out of his jacket pocket. It looked just like the one I had in my hand.

"You wrote a letter?" I managed. "So did I."

His grin got even wider. "Really?"

I nodded, realizing there were tears in my eyes. "Yeah."

He closed the gap between us, brushing my hair out of my face. "I had to do something. I couldn't let you go."

I smiled at the familiar gesture. "I missed you," I said, blinking back tears. He had been thinking about me too.

He blew out a breath, making fog rise in the air. "I missed you too." He paused, then went on. "What about the suit and beard, though?" he asked. "Do you miss that?"

I laughed, taking in his appearance without the red velvet suit and realistic white beard. From his blonde wavy hair to his thick coat and blue jeans. The slight pink in his cheeks from the cold. "You did pull off that long beard pretty well," I quipped.

He took my hand. "Maybe I can talk the committee into letting me borrow it sometime."

Then he bent down and kissed me. His lips were warm, his nose cold as it brushed over my cheeks. His arms wrapped around my waist, and I easily settled my hands on his shoulders. My heart fluttered as my body remembered our kiss outside the theater. This was him. It was really him.

I smiled up at him in awe. "So, the committee decided to grant you an exception?" I asked.

"Maybe they saw what I did. That I wanted *us* to be a part of the magic."

## 29
## NICK

It was New Year's Eve.

After a long sleigh ride with Belle around town, cuddled under a thick red blanket, we were ready to warm back up.

We made our way hand in hand toward Cocoa Corner for some hot chocolate. I knew it was her favorite, and it was starting to be mine too. Even though it had been less than two weeks, it felt like so long ago that we sat together in the coffee shop, getting to know each other.

As we passed the Christmas tree, we couldn't help but stop and gaze up at it. The lights had gone from sparkling red, green, and gold to just gold in honor of the new year. It was a sight to behold, especially with Belle on my arm.

I couldn't believe everything had worked out, although my mom could. She was so happy for me, and I loved that she was the kind of person who never lost faith, even after everything she'd been through.

Even though she deserved so much more.

"I'm going to be sad to see it gone," Belle said quietly.

"Me too," I replied, looking over at her, the gold lights reflecting in her eyes.

After a moment, we kept walking. The sun had set not long ago, and the plan was to meet my mom later at Scrooge's. She wanted to meet Belle, and I couldn't wait for them to see each other. I knew they'd get along.

"You know," Belle said, giving my hand a squeeze, "I made a wish this year, at the star ceremony. But I really didn't think it would come true."

I thought about that for a second. "Did it?"

She stopped at the corner between Cider Center and Cocoa Corner and smiled up at me. "Yeah, I think it did."

"Well, as it turns out, I made a wish too," I admitted.

She gave me a small smile. Everyone in Garland

made a wish, whether you believed it could come true or not. "What was it?"

I brushed back a piece of hair that had escaped from her braid. "To be seen for who I really am, beyond all the external stuff."

She nodded in understanding. "And then you ended up in the Santa suit."

"Crazy, huh?" I said.

"Good crazy," she replied with a smile. Then her face flashed with awe. "Wow, Garland wishes do come true."

Almost as if on cue, soft white snowflakes fluttered down to the ground all around us.

It reminded me of the first time we kissed. It made me want to kiss her again, so I did.

When we made it to Cocoa Corner, we found that it was closed.

"Come on," I said. "Let's head to Scrooge's. I'll buy you a milkshake instead. And we can see how Scrooge is doing too before my mom comes along and gets him all flustered."

"Scrooge gets flustered?" Belle asked.

I smirked. "You'd be surprised."

I texted Mom, letting her know where she could find us, only to find her already at Scrooge's, sitting at our usual spot at the counter.

She appeared to be talking Scrooge's ear off, and he looked like he didn't mind.

"Is it me, or is Scrooge looking sort of happy for the first time ever?" Belle told me.

We began making our way over to the counter but then I stopped, not wanting to ruin the moment for them. "I think you're right. They both seem happy."

"And what do you think about that?" she asked.

I knew what she was really asking—if I was okay with my mom dating again. "Honestly, if he makes Mom happy, that's all that matters."

She gave my hand a squeeze. "Maybe she can convince him to finally shave off that scruff. I bet he looks pretty handsome under there."

I grinned at her. "Coming from someone who couldn't get enough of mine."

That made her laugh.

Then we made our way over to Scrooge and Mom, enjoying just another piece of the magic in Garland.

RETURN TO GARLAND with more holiday romance stories in the Curvy Girl Christmas series!

## AUTHOR'S NOTE

A few years ago, I released a Curvy Girl Christmas box. The featured item inside was a red sweater with the phrase "Santa Loves Curvy Girls." Those words stood out to me throughout the years, and I knew I had to do something more with them than a sweater; they would be the perfect title for a book.

So now that I had a title, I knew I had to come up with a story to match. Ha! (Or should I say Ho! Ho! Ho! lol)

My mind started spinning about Santa and Christmas and romance and a love story I hadn't seen before. I daydreamed about a magical place where wishes came true and special traditions were held sacred amongst a close-knit community.

## AUTHOR'S NOTE

And I imagined what it would be like to grow up in a place like that.

Would you be put off by all the Christmassy things? Or would you love it?

For Belle, the answer was obvious. She adored Garland and all things Christmas. Just like she adored making cookies.

I think Belle was one of the most fun characters to write in this entire series because of how purely she loved things. She didn't hold back from her passions, even though others might have thought of them as silly hobbies or juvenile fascinations. The truth is, people like Belle are my favorite people—those who are unabashedly interested in something and share those interests with others.

I love watching people light up when they talk about something that interests and delights them. You can see all their features come to life, their eyes practically sparkle, and they just look like they feel lighter than they did before.

Have you ever felt like that? So passionate and energized about a new interest or hobby?

I certainly have. About totally random things too—there was the sourdough phase where I learned everything there was to know about sourdough starters and gifted everyone I knew with sourdough cinnamon rolls and sagging sourdough loafs. How about that time I became a certified yoga teacher just for fun? Or the phase where I dove deep into DIY and learning how to improve our home inspired by all the people I saw doing the same on Insta. There's also been... cake baking, cookie decorating, gardening, animal husbandry and more!

I think learning new skills and leaning into your interests is part of what makes life fun and enriching.

We're coming up on the time of year when people are going to be throwing resolution ideas your way. And let's be honest, it's going to be diet companies screaming from the rooftops for you to lose weight.

But that's not all there is!

What if you made a goal to go all in on one of your interests this year like Belle did with baking? How much better would your life be with a fun new hobby you never took seriously before? Could you meet new friends who share the same interests? Find new travel opportunities to learn more about your hobby and explore more of the world?

AUTHOR'S NOTE

Letting yourself love something like Belle does could bring so much joy and fun to the new year. And if you have a cute Santa to share it with? Even better. ;)

# ACKNOWLEDGMENTS

Thank you so much to everyone who made my first Christmas series a possibility!

Team Kelsie for having my back and helping me have time to write and be creative!

Sally, my bestie, and a leader on Team Kelsie, for always being a shoulder to lean on as well as a kick in the pants when I need it!

My husband, Ty, for letting me bounce ideas off him and share my excitement for this story well outside of the Christmas season!

My kids had fun helping me come up with names and will surely help out when it comes time to sign and share these books with you, dear reader!

My cover designer, Najla Qamber at Qamber Designs, took my idea and made it a million times better. (As per usual. ;)

My editor, Tricia, made me so happy with her encouraging comments as I got outside of my comfort zone with this story.

Jordan, my proofreader, used her eye for detail to help these stories be as error-free as possible!

Courtney and Luke for giving the story fabulous narration so you can listen on the go during the busy Christmas season!

My brother/audio editor Dakota Hoss, gives me the ability to record the author's notes and acknowledgements so you can hear this in my own voice!

The readers in Kelsie Stelting: Reader's Club for being endlessly kind and supportive of all things in the Kelsie-verse!

And also, you, sweet reader. I'm so thankful you took the time to read this story and my words at the end. I wrote this for you.

# ABOUT THE AUTHOR

Kelsie Stelting is a body positive romance author who writes love stories with strong characters, deep feelings, and happy endings.

She currently lives in Colorado with her family. You can often find her writing, spending time with family, and soaking up too much sun wherever she can find it.

**Hang out with Kelsie in her online readers' group!**

facebook.com/kelsiesteltingcreative
instagram.com/kelsiestelting

ALSO BY KELSIE STELTING

### **The Curvy Girl Club**

Curvy Girls Can't Date Quarterbacks

Curvy Girls Can't Date Billionaires

Curvy Girls Can't Date Cowboys

Curvy Girls Can't Date Bad Boys

Curvy Girls Can't Date Best Friends

Curvy Girls Can't Date Bullies

Curvy Girls Can't Dance

Curvy Girls Can't Date Soldiers

Curvy Girls Can't Date Princes

Curvy Girls Can't Date Rock Stars

Curvy Girls Can't Date Surfers

Curvy Girls Can't Date Point Guards

Curvy Girls Can't Date Curvy Girls (Pride Edition)

### **The Texas High Series**

Chasing Skye

Becoming Skye

Loving Skye

Always Anika

## New at Texas High

Abi and the Boy Next Door

Abi and the Boy Who Lied

Abi and the Boy She Loves

## The Pen Pal Romance Series

Dear Adam

Fabio Vs. the Friend Zone

Sincerely Cinderella

## Standalone YA Romance

Road Trip with the Enemy

## YA Contemporary Romance Anthologies

The Art of Taking Chances

Two More Days

## Nonfiction

Raising the West